A Harry Circus Mystery

# NIGHT HUNTER

*By E.D. Ward*

To Ron,

Enjoy the Downeast flare!

Laurie Y. Barsalou

for

E.D. Ward

1950 - 2016

*Night Hunter*
Copyright 2017 E.D. Ward

Published by Piscataqua Press
An imprint of RiverRun Bookstore, Inc.
142 Fleet Street | Portsmouth, NH | 03801
www.riverrunbookstore.com
www.piscataquapress.com
ISBN: 978-1-944393-41-0
Printed in the United States of America

*This book is dedicated to my entire family for
their patience and support—mostly Lou,
who continued to type on snowy, winter days,
and maintained the constant belief that I would
finish when I so often proclaimed I could not.
Thanks, Kevin, and thank you, Kelly,
for your invaluable assistance.*

*PREFACE*

*Bangor Daily News,* August 21, 1978. The body of a prominent local banker from Berryville, found on a deserted woods road in western Washington County, has left area residents shocked. According to an unnamed State Police spokesperson, details are sketchy, but the victim, tied to a makeshift codfish drying rack, was disemboweled and partially skinned. State Police are intensifying their investigation in the small surrounding towns.

## PROLOGUE

JUNE 7, 1967. An unusually cold rain fell heavily on the entire Down East area, forcing mostly everyone inside to the comfort of their wood heat. Dim lights showed through the curtained windows of the small house. The large, black luxury car parked beside it seemed out of place. The sound of madness from within bled slightly through the thin walls, muffled by the heavy pelting rain against the roof. The struggle lasted only a short time, until his strength overpowered her.

She lay beneath him, injured, unable to push him away any longer. His face reflected the violence he had inflicted on this innocent woman. What he did not know was that he was being watched. Emotionally scarred for life, another innocent victim sat quietly in horror, trembling, eyes wide in fear, silenced only by the physical inability to scream. The child, knowing very well who this lunatic was, sat in the darkness of a closet through an evening of hell that seemed to last an eternity.

## CHAPTER 1

---

T HE BEAT-UP OLD JEEP WAGONEER labored to climb the hill that led to what the locals called "The Bog" in the small town of Berryville, Maine. Still a very rural area, it would soon feel the ravages of the woodsman's ax. As the old Jeep clambered along the gravel, Pat driving as usual, Marge sat in the rear seat lighting matches, flipping them with the tip of her forefinger across the striker, into the ashtray on the opposite door, and more frequently, onto the floor of the Jeep. She kept her favorite 30/30 Winchester by her side, and as always, the six-pack of Bud on the floor.

Pat and Marge had been together nearly seven years, ever since Marge's father, Harvey, had died of pneumonia, leaving her unable to care for herself. Most folks from the area couldn't understand why Pat volunteered to take her in, but Pat had a secret that bound her to him for life. They were, in every sense of the word, total opposites. Pat, a strong-willed loner, never allowed anyone to do anything for her, and never offered to do anything for anyone. Marge, who many people thought was slow, had been diagnosed with Intermittent Explosive Disorder, a condition that thrust an individual into episodes of uncontrollable aggressive impulses, often resulting in the destruction of property. Marge always wore her bibbed jeans and faded T-shirt. Because of her thin frame, her clothes always seemed too big on her, but they never got in the way. Her slender features were accentuated with the ever present, boy-like haircut. Pat, seemingly in a trance while driving, fantasized a sexual encounter with Jimmy White. Just thinking of the two of them together gave her a tingle. Pat hated to ask Jimmy over—she knew how he felt about Marge.

Jimmy could not stand the way she stared at him with her deep-set and stabbing eyes. He knew the stories about her and the old men in town. Some had probably been made up by the boys at the lower corner convenience store, but he knew that some were true. The favorite cut-up that he always said under his breath each time he saw her was, *"She didn't get those lips from suckin' popsicles."*

"Sometimes I want her out of my life so bad," Pat thought to herself, not realizing she was whispering.

"Were you talking to me, little Pat bitch?" She did not mean bitch in a derogatory way. They simply called each other bitch occasionally.

"Be quiet, Marge! Can't you see I'm driving?"

"I want to kill something," Marge exclaimed. "I want to kill something, I want to kill something!"

"Please," screeched Pat, but to no avail. Marge just continued. Her mind seemed to leave the ground whenever she got in this mood with a fever to kill. Pat knew what it would be like until Marge was able to kill something—anything—a porcupine, a raccoon, a dog. The chant would continue until she killed. "I want to kill something, I want to kill something, I want to kill something." They were almost to the bog now, usually a good place to kill something. From the back seat the chanting continued, dropping Pat into deeper anxiety, her breathing labored. The thought of just blowing Marge away seemed like it would be a very easy thing to do. Even though it was a very dark night, from the corner of one eye Pat saw the reflection of eyes as the headlight's beam illuminated the corner of a blueberry field.

"There, you bitch! There's something to kill."

"Where?" Marge asked.

"Wait!" Pat reached for the spotlight on the seat beside her, and switched it on in the direction of the eyes.

"Big buck," slurred Marge, drooling with the formation of the words. She aimed her cocked and ready rifle out the window. **Boom!** The explosion from the muzzle and the ensuing spit of flame shot out of the rear side window of the Jeep as the deer fell like a sack of potatoes.

—

"Good morning, is Harry home?" The gravelly voice of Walter Grant, who lived up on Route 193, echoed from the receiver. "I'd like to speak with him, please."

"Whom may I say is calling?" asked Annie, the wife of State Trooper Harry Circus, in her soft, mild voice.

"This is Walter up on 193. I need to talk to him right away, it's important!" Annie had known Walter since she was a little girl, when her family lived by the river. It seemed funny that as close as Walter had been to her father back then, he would not acknowledge more than just good morning to her now. Her soft blue eyes turned slowly toward the dining room table where Harry seemed to be enjoying his morning coffee. From the look on his face, she knew that whatever Walter thought important would more than likely be trivial, and not go over very big with Harry this morning. He was the only trooper in the area. He and the town's constable were the only law for many miles. A call to a trooper, in most cases, was taken seriously.

"Harry, it's Walter up on 193, he says it's important."

Harry squinted. He shook his head as he sent Annie a very disgusted look, and said softly, "Shit, shit, shit! What a great way to start the day!" Annie, holding the phone in her outstretched hand as she watched her husband walk toward her, thought to herself that he still looked as good as when she'd fallen in love with him in high school. "*Nice body!*" she thought. "*I just wish he would let his hair grow a little longer.*" As she handed him the phone, she kissed his cheek, then walked to the kitchen to finish cooking breakfast.

"This is Harry! What's up, Walter?"

"Harry, you got to stop the goddamned shootin' up here at night, I can't get no sleep!"

"What shooting, Walter?"

"The goddamned shootin' goin' on in the goddamned rud'. Someone's shootin' all the goddamned rud' signs off their goddamned poles."

"Settle down, Walter. I'm sure it's not as bad as all that."

"They shot the goddamned sign right in front of my house last night, and don't think that didn't stir my shit up." Harry rolled his eyes toward the ceiling and took his final gulp of coffee.

"Alright, Walter, I'll be up that way around midday—think you'll be home?"

"Well, I don't goddamned know where else I'd be but here."

"Well, okay, I'll be up, see you then." Harry hung the receiver in its cradle. Walking to the kitchen, he called out to Annie, "Let's run away!" Annie just smiled as she continued to toss the scrambled eggs.

"You know," Harry continued, "Walter's okay but I think he's starting to go downhill. Do you know what I mean, Annie?"

"I know, Harry. As he's gotten older, he just seems to be a little unsure of himself. She picked up a plate to place the eggs on. "I know I wouldn't want to live out there by myself. Try to be a little patient with him."

"Sure," Harry said.

—

Pat and Marge were just driving into town as Trooper Circus sat down for breakfast. In the back of the Jeep, covered neatly with the blue tarp, was the big buck deer that Marge had shot several hours before. Entering town from this direction brought them directly by Harry Circus' house. Marge noticed him sitting at his window seat, and hollered "Hey asshole! Guess what we got under the tarp?" The windows of the house were closed, so he never heard Marge's voice.

"Shut up," hissed Pat. "You'll get us locked up yet."

"Don't you worry, little Pat bitch. I'll kill that son of a bitch if he comes near us."

"Ya, right!" Pat said. "Just keep your mouth shut and everything will be fine."

"Oh, ya! Little Pat bitch, I'll just keep my mouth shut and everything will be just fine, just fine." Pat said nothing; she stared straight ahead and drove the Jeep up the gravel drive that led to their cabin by the river, one mile from Harry's place.

## CHAPTER 2

LESTER SAWYER WALKED INTO THE BANK at one minute after nine. Darcy looked up and greeted him as she did every morning, with a lovely smile and a gracious good-morning greeting.

"Good morning, Darcy, beautiful day, isn't it?"

Darcy did not respond. She nodded her head and kept smiling. She watched him as he walked toward his office, and wondered how a nit-wit like him ever got to be a bank's branch manager. She smiled and said softly to herself. "Oh well, I guess it's not what you know."

—

Lester sat at his desk, and as usual, his coffee was brought to him by his favorite teller, Irene. He liked Irene a lot.

"Good morning, Lester," Irene said. "Here's your coffee, nice and hot the way you love it."

"Ooh, thank you, my dear." Looking to see that no one was

watching, he said, "Come closer; let me give you a little pinch."

"Oh, Lester, you're so fresh." She giggled, then moved closer.

He was reaching for her when Darcy appeared at the opened door of Lester's office, cleared her throat, and said, "Excuse me, Lester?"

"Yes, my dear, what can I do for you?"

"Lester, you told me to remind you this morning when you arrived that you wanted to see me."

"Oh, yes, please come in and be seated." The heat of jealousy flared through Irene's body. If she knew Lester—and she did—his little mind was probably thinking of how he would arrange to have cute, little Darcy bring him his morning coffee. She thought, "*I would like to...*" Just then, Lester looked toward Irene. "Would you please excuse us? But when Darcy leaves, I'd like to get to the bottom of the conversation we'd started."

Irene let her breath out. "Of course, Lester." She walked out, closing the door behind her.

Lester folded his hands and started. "Darcy, you've been with us here at the bank about what, a year now?" He took a large gulp from the coffee.

"It will be a year next week," she said.

"Well, I feel that you are rapidly becoming my most favorite teller, and you know I always take good care of my favorite tellers." "*Oh...great,*" she thought. "*Instead of a raise, this little fat guy is going to try to put the make on me.*"

"Well, Darcy," Lester began, "I think it's time we gave you a little more compensation for your dedication. Let me just look through your file, and while I'm doing that, why don't you be a good girl and fix me another cup of coffee, two sugars and extra cream, dear."

As Darcy walked toward the table, she could feel his eyes all over her. "*If he touches me when I bring him this coffee...*" Lester's eyes moved from top to bottom, scanning Darcy as she returned with the hot coffee. "You look beautiful today, my dear. Is that a new dress?" *"Here it comes,"* she thought. She came around the side of the desk to place the cup next to him. His fat, little hand ended up on her knee, lifting her dress ever so slightly.

The scream that came from Lester's office was enough to make the teller's cash drawers open by themselves. As Irene ran into the office, she found Darcy apologizing nervously and dabbing the top of Lester's bald head with the towel that they kept on the coffee table. Irene began to laugh quite loudly as Lester's face took on the appearance of a freshly boiled Maine lobster.

"I'll be fine" Lester said, grimacing. "Both of you, please, leave me and close the door on your way."

—

Over at the corner variety store, William Bradley was restocking the ammunition shelves. He was dressed in his usual torn blue jeans and faded T-shirt. "I just can't understand where all that 30/30 ammo goes. Seems I just stocked this shelf last few days, and already it's gone." He was muttering to himself, not realizing that Pat and Marge had walked in and were standing behind him on the customer side of the counter.

"Hey, William!" Marge hollered. At that, William nearly fell off his step-stool.

"Don't do that, Marge, you damn near give me a heart attack!"

"What a dumbass!" Marge said, looking for a response from Pat. Pat simply looked down at the shiny new pistols inside the glass display case in front of her.

"Can I do something for you ladies?" William emphasized the word "ladies."

"Yeah, why don't you give me a couple of those boxes of 30/30's there, you big dumbshit," Marge ordered.

"Look! I don't have to take that from you, retard!" As soon as the words were out of his mouth, Marge leaped over the counter, grabbing William by the collar, shaking him as if she would break his neck.

"Christ, almighty," Pat said, upon hearing the scuffle, and ran to try to break it up. She knew the two hated each other, and Marge had often talked about killing William just for the fun of it.

The noise that the scuffle caused brought several store employees and a customer to see what was happening. Pat was tugging at Marge's arms, trying to break them apart as William kept screaming, "Get this retard off me! Get this retard off of me! I'm calling Harry Circus. He'll take care of you, retard!" It took Pat several minutes to calm William down, and everything she had to get Marge into the Jeep.

Once they were in the Jeep, she cried, "Christ almighty! Are you trying to get us arrested or something?"

Marge kept repeating, "I'm sorry, Pat. I'm sorry, Pat. I just don't like it when someone calls me a retard, I just don't like it."

"I know, but you're going to get us arrested."

—

Walter was looking out his kitchen window when the trooper car stopped out front. Walter's place wasn't much more than a tarpaper shack, but it had become quite a landmark on this seldom-traveled road through the woods. Most folks from Berryville would take the Black Bear Road if they were going to Bangor. Traffic around here was an occasional log truck or hunters. Harry hadn't been to Walter's in years, but nothing had changed. Walter greeted him at the door and invited him in.

Walking through the door, to his left was the old cast-iron

cook stove, and across from it—not three feet away—was the antique dining room table that took up most of the floor space. Dishes and canned goods exposed on shelves without doors filled one entire side of the room. Across from the door and over to his right was a doorway that led to the woodshed.

"Sit down, Harry, sit down, have a cup of coffee." Harry looked at his watch. It was 12:15 p.m., just around midday. Walter was pouring him a cup. "How do you want it, Harry, a little milk, sugar?"

"Just the way you pour it will be fine, Walter."

Walter immediately began speaking. "Now Harry, I want you to know I'm not some little old granny complaining about a little noise after dark. I'm not scared of anything or anybody, but I get to sleep these days and hate being woke up with gunshots." Harry was letting Walter rant on so he might finish his coffee.

"Uh, huh," Harry said, fidgeting.

"Now, one more thing. I want you to take a look at that sign over there 'cross the rud'. That's what woke me up, Harry. They shot that sign."

"Did you see who did it, Walter?"

"Well, if I goddamned knew that I woulda' called them insteada' you." Harry kept drinking his coffee, and kind of rolled his eyes back in his head.

"I bet you would have, Walter." Harry hurried to finish his coffee as the old man rattled on about the little things that went on in the small town. Finally, Harry said, "Okay, let's take a look at that sign, Walter."

"Ya, let's go." Walter grabbed his hat and they crossed the road. "See that, Harry? Two quick shots right close to the middle."

"I can see that, but are you sure these were made from the same shooting?"

"Goddamned right I am. Pop...pop...one...two. I heard it."

15

Harry thought that whoever it was that shot the sign had to be a good shot, or just plain lucky. The two holes in the sign were very close, and considering the speed of a moving vehicle, that was some damned good shooting.

"Looks like 30/30 to me, Harry."

—

After they finished cutting and wrapping the deer meat upon their return from the corner variety, Marge went out alone to sit on the big boulder that rested half in and half out of the river. She often sat there watching the river passing swiftly around the large rock and thinking about the days when Harvey was still alive. She could picture them hunting the ridges whenever they needed meat, or setting up their nets so the game wardens would go right by them, never knowing anything was in the water.

On summer nights, they would sit on the step gazing at the stars, listening to the night sounds around them, smoking their pipes until late in the evening. "Life was good then." Marge was talking to herself again. "I'd like to go back up river with Harvey, life was good then, but you dropped that big buck though, right Marge? Yes, you did."

It was dark now, and the total black of the sky exposed a billion stars. Marge looked up, puffing away as her pipe bellowed out twisting columns of smoke. "And you'll get an even bigger buck next time, Marge girl," she said aloud.

## CHAPTER 3

---

JIMMY WHITE WAS KIND OF A LONER when it came to his private life. When he was in a crowd, however, Jimmy was quite a mixer. He would be first in line when it came time for pranks, and he was all ears when there was a new joke being told. He stood about six feet tall, and was somewhat lanky in appearance, but if one looked closely, his broad shoulders gave him a rather rugged look. Those that knew him well also knew he could swing a mean splitting maul, as he split all of his winter firewood needs with one. He was in his late twenties now, and feeling more and more the need to find himself a good woman. "Someone like Pat would be nice," he would say to friends during morning coffee breaks at the lower corner Quick-Stop. He also felt that Pat might just feel the same way about him. There was only one problem, MARGE! He could get along with anyone, but the hardest thing he had ever done was try, for Pat's sake, to get along with Marge.

The afternoon shadows were high as Jimmy's firewood-laden truck stopped in front of Walter's cabin. Before the engine had stopped, Walter appeared in the open doorway, and seemed to be scolding Jimmy for being late. However, the smile in the corners of his eyes gave him away. "Well, what's the goddamned excuse this time? You said you'd be here early."

"Well, it's not dark yet, is it?" Jimmy asked.

"No, I guess not. Want some coffee?"

"Sure," said Jimmy, and walked into the cabin behind Walter. "I heard tell there's been some shootin' up here at night—you night-huntin', old man?"

"No, goddammit, I ain't night-huntin' up here or anywhere else, but someone goddamned near made me jump out of my shorts, though. Someone shot that sign 'cross the way with a 30/30."

"Wicked! I bet that made a hell of a bang."

"I guess it made a goddamned bang. How'd you want this coffee, Jimmy?"

"Oh, just one sugar will be fine, Walter." They sat together and just small-talked for a while, making Walter very happy. Jimmy watched the old man's lips moving, only half-listening to what he was saying. Just then, Walter stood up quickly.

"Come on, Jimmy, I'll show you that sign 'cross the rud', then I'll show you where I want that wood."

"Sure," Jimmy said. As they were leaving the cabin, their attention was on the Jeep Wagoneer traveling at a high rate of speed toward them. Jimmy almost split his upper lip smiling when he realized that it was Pat's Wagoneer.

The very moment Jimmy recognized Pat, she recognized him. She brought the Jeep to a smoky, rumbling stop along the shoulder. "Hi, Jimmy!"

"Hi, Pat, what are you two doin' up hea' this time of day?"

Pat wondered what he might think if she came right out and said, *"Oh we're trying to find something to kill,"* but instead she said, "Riding around, thought we might go out to camp for a while."

The camp was where Harvey and Marge used to live, and had been left to Marge when he died. The two of them kept it as neat and clean as it always was. That's the way Harvey always wanted it.

Walter was looking through the Jeep as Pat and Jimmy exchanged small talk, unaware of Marge's observant eyes, watching every move he made from the passenger side of the rear seat. "Say," Walter asked, "is that a 30/30 you got theya'?"

"Yeah, what of it?" Marge sneered.

"Were you two up hea' shootin' the other night?" At the sound of that question, Pat thought she had swallowed her tongue.

"What's that you said, Walter?"

From the back seat, Marge hollered. "You go shit in your socks...you old bastard, Walter, you old bastard, Walter!"

"Christ almighty," Pat said, and started the Jeep's engine.

"Well, listen," Jimmy said, "think we can go to the dance on Friday night?"

"Maybe," replied Pat. "I'll see you tomorrow down at the Quick-Stop and we'll talk about it."

"Sure," Jimmy said as Pat squealed the tires and sped away.

"I don't know about them two, Jimmy. I don't trust that Marge, she's...."

Jimmy interrupted him. "Where'd you say you wanted that wood, Walter?"

—

Davis Norton was pumping gas into the old school bus when trooper Circus pulled up at the pump opposite him. "Afternoon Harry," Davis said, pulling the lock tab on the nozzle and walking over to Harry's car.

"What's been happening with you, Davis? I haven't seen you in weeks."

19

"Not much, Harry, just now gettin' the bus and all ready to start school again."

"Oh, yeah, where the hell did summer go?"

All Davis said was "Ayah!" Davis Norton, besides being the school bus driver for the last fifteen years, was one of the best fly-tiers Down East. He was a big man with large hands. Most people would ask how it was that a man with such large hands could stand doing such tight, tedious work. He'd usually giggle an "ayah" and say, "Oh these large fingers have been in a lot of tight places, ayah."

Davis spent much of his time totally enjoying the out-of-doors, sitting in his boat casting a line or standing in waders snatching brook trout from the streams and brooks throughout the Down East area. Because of his passion for the out-of-doors, the law of averages delivered him to that certain place at that certain time. He had been parked less than a quarter mile away from the spot where Marge had dropped the big buck, making it possible to hear the report from her rifle.

Given the time of the shot, and the location, Davis Norton just stayed right where he was. He knew what was happening: it was a poacher, and there was no way he was getting any closer to where that shot had come from. That night, he would definitely mind his business. After all, people needed to eat, and he'd be neither judge nor jury, and even less a witness against a poacher. He stayed parked down by the boat launch when he heard the rumble of the poacher's engine starting in the distance. He listened as the vehicle clambered down the gravel road, and strained to hear its rumble fade into the dark night. Then and only then did he attempt to start his engine and leave in the opposite direction. The extra fifteen miles home just wasn't at all important that night.

Harry was about to get out of his car when the thought hit him that Davis was usually on top of most gossip and local news.

"Say, Davis, have you heard that old Walter up on 193 might be slipping a little lately?"

"How do you mean slippin', Harry?"

"Well, you know, his mind starting to go with age."

"No, I haven't Harry. Why, is he gettin' to be a pest or somethin'?"

"No, not exactly that," Harry said. "I just...never mind, it's not important."

"Whatever you say, Harry. Catch ya' layta," Davis said as he jumped into the school bus, waiting for the tank to fill.

Harry looked up as he saw the first drop of rain fall onto the windshield of his cruiser. "Shit, looks like tonight might be a good night to stay home."

—

Pat was very concerned with Marge's embittered attitude toward people. *"Here we are,"* she thought, *"driving back out to the woods because Marge wanted to kill something."* Thinking about the incident at the variety store with William the previous day, the thing with Walter a few minutes before, she realized that on several occasions lately Marge had become very aggressive with her. *"No, this is crazy! I have nothing to fear,"* she thought. *"Marge wouldn't do anything to hurt me. After all, I've brought her to my home, taken care of her all these years. She'd never hurt me."*

At that very moment, Marge shoved the 30/30 out the window of the Jeep, and fired three shots at the road sign on the shoulder. Pat kept staring straight ahead, with mixed feelings of uncertainty and fear. Marge, laughing like one possessed, kept repeating, "I know I hit it, little Pat, I know I hit it." After a few miles of silence, Marge exclaimed, "Say, little Pat, this is not the way to the bog now, is it?"

"No way. I have no intention of going back down there after being there the other night. We're going in the opposite direction, thank you—I just don't feel like going to jail tonight, do you?"

21

"Hell… no, little Pat. No one is going to jail tonight, hell no."

"Well then, why don't you leave your rifle and six-pack and jump in the front. We'll be turning down the road I want, soon now."

"Okay, little Pat, I'll get in the front." When Marge reached the front seat, taking one beer with her, she took her usual low crouch, and popped the beer and began guzzling the brew. The now-familiar chant came between swallows. "I want to kill something, I want to kill something." Pat, shaking her head slightly, kept driving. It had been raining for about fifteen minutes when Pat turned onto the gravel road.

The sky unleashed a downpour, making the driving almost impossible. Pat gripped the wheel and leaned forward, trying to get a better look at the road. Marge scrambled back to the rear seat, popped the second beer, and the chanting began to drive Pat completely out of her mind. "Will you please shut up, Marge?"

"Please shut…uuup," sang Marge.

"Christ almighty," Pat said quietly, "If she doesn't shut up, I'm going to go out of my mind." Chills began to run up the back of Pat's neck when the chanting stopped and Marge injected three new rounds to replace the ones she'd fired at the road sign. It was as if she was unable to move at the wheel.

"What are you doing, Marge?"

"I forgot to re-load my rifle, little Pat. If I don't have any bullets in my gun, I can't kill anything, I can't kill anything."

It seemed as though they had been driving forever; but actually, it had only been an hour since they'd left the paved road. The rain was still coming down heavily, but at least it had lightened up a little. Pat was able to drive at a normal speed, and was somewhat more relaxed now, except in regard to Marge's chanting.

They were approaching the area called King's Corner. It was some distance from the tar road in a vast open area known as the barrens. Pat took them in another direction from her original plan for camp. Ahead of them, she could see, faintly through the still, driving rain, a pickup truck off to the side of the road. Not knowing who it might be, she reached for the spotlight in its usual place on the front seat and quickly placed it between her legs under the seat. Spotlights, or jacklights as they are called, are considered illegal in Maine especially when used for night hunting. As they approached, she recognized the blue pickup and its occupant—old Lennie from town, probably too drunk to drive, passed out at the wheel. Pat blasted the horn and revved the motor, but Lennie never moved.

"Maybe he's dead," Marge said.

"Just sit tight, I'll check it out," Pat said and got out of the Jeep.

"You check it out, little Pat, you check it out." Approaching the pickup, she could see the generator light, indicating that possibly, the engine had stalled. She gave Lennie a nudge, nothing. Her heart went to her throat. His face was pale and wrinkled with the deep grooves of weathered skin of one who'd spent the seasons of his life outdoors. Smoking and excessive drinking gave him the appearance of someone ten years older than his actual age.

"Oh shit, he is dead," she whispered. She immediately began shaking him.

Lennie moaned, "Leave me the fuck alone." Pat passed her hand across her forehead, relieved at hearing the old man's voice.

"Hang in there, Lennie," she said, returning to the Jeep, a little wet.

"What's his problem?" Marge asked. "Looks like a little too much beer to me. I'll show him how to drink beer," and with that Marge threw an empty into the back of Lennie's pickup and popped another one. Pat got into the Jeep and started the engine, but stayed parked alongside Lennie's pickup. She reached under the seat, grabbing the spotlight and replacing it in its usual spot on the seat beside her. Through her rear-view mirror, Pat caught a slight movement, and moved her head to get a better look. What she saw caused her heart to pound heavily, like the feeling you'd get as the big bass drum passed at a parade. The horror of what she now saw in the reflection left her numb and unable to move in fear for her own safety.

Sitting in the back seat, Marge had leveled the rifle, finger on the trigger, in the direction of Lennie's head as he slumped over the wheel. "Marge, what in hell are you doing?" Pat screeched. Startled, Marge jumped, then lowered the rifle. She stared at Pat with deep-set eyes, and a look of brutal dissatisfaction crossed her face. For the very first time, Pat was unsure of what would happen next.

"What is your problem, little Pat bitch? Did you think I was gonna' shoot that old fart?"

Trembling, Pat responded with, "I...I'm not sure, you had a funny look about you, and I just didn't know what you were gonna do. Marge, I think maybe you might be drinking too much lately!"

"Oh, my... little Pat bitch wants to be my mother now."

"No, that's not it, Marge. I'm concerned for your welfare, that's all."

"Now little Pat bitch sounds like those assholes down at the welfare office. We're only concerned for your welfare. We're only concerned for your welfare. Say, Pat, what do you think it would be like if I popped him in the head?"

"Now you're talking stupid, Marge, ya know that?"

"We've been driving around here for hours and I haven't killed anything yet."

"Well, goddammit, you're not gonna kill Lennie. He's never done anything to you." Marge threw another empty into the back of Lennie's truck and opened another beer. Upon hearing the beer open, Pat shifted into gear and pulled away quickly, while Marge still had both hands on the can.

"Pat, you didn't answer my question, dea'. What do you think it would be like if I'd popped old Lennie in the head back theya'?"

"I don't want to think about it, Marge!" Pat pulled the Jeep to a stop. "Marge, leave the rifle in back and come sit up front with me."

"Sure," Marge said. Reaching for her last two beers, she placed the rifle on the back seat, then jumped into the front. They drove for several more miles over some of the most rough, rock-exposed road that they'd been on in a long time. Marge eventually complained, "This road sucks, Pat. When we gonna' be off it?"

"Soon, Marge, we should be close to the tar. If I remember right, it's about a mile ahead."

## CHAPTER 4

PAT AWOKE TO THE NUMBNESS OF FEAR still embedded in her mind from her experience with Marge the evening before. It all kept coming back in cloudy but all-too-vivid visions. She could not believe that Marge had leveled the rifle at Lennie. She wanted to think that it was all a nasty joke, but the look in Marge's eyes kept stabbing her soul. "Christ, Lennie never hurt anyone, he just loves gettin' smashed," she said softly.

At that moment, Marge walked in with an armload of thin birch sticks for the cook stove as Pat came in from her room just off the kitchen. "Mornin'...little Pat."

"Good morning, Marge. You're out early this morning." While speaking, Pat noticed the orange line of sunrise forming at the base of the tall pines through the clearing.

"Ya, I'm hungry this morning, Pat. I didn't kill anything last night, you know." Pat was dumbfounded that the first thoughts in Marge's mind were food and killing.

"Marge, don't you ever think of anything else?"

"Not...usually, little Pat." Pat had made her way across the kitchen and was sitting in the rocking chair by the window, diagonally across the room from the wood cook stove. The fire, which Marge had started earlier, crackled when she added the thin birch sticks through one of the round covers on the stove. The coffee was hot, and Marge poured a cup and brought it to Pat.

"Thank you, Marge."

"You're welcome, little Pat. Would you like some eggs and toast this morning? I'm cooking."

"No, thanks. I'm going down to the Quick-Stop as soon as I drink this coffee. I'd like to meet Jimmy this morning when he stops."

"I'll go with you, Pat."

"No!" And, as the word passed her lips, she realized how it must have sounded: like an order as opposed to a reply.

"Well, I guess you mean no, don't you, little Pat bitch?"

"I'm sorry, Marge, I didn't mean I don't want you to come with me, but Jimmy and I have something to talk about, and you know how..."

"Oh...yah," Marge interrupted. "He thinks I'm a retard!"

Pat stood up, "It's no use. I can see I'm getting nowhere with you today. Marge, you stay here and cook your breakfast. I'll be back before you're finished eating, and we'll go fishing or something."

"That's great, that's great," Marge said. "I'll have everything ready when you get back."

The old Jeep started with a rumble that echoed through the stillness of the surrounding woods. Pat steered the Jeep in a circle around a pile of wood stacked in the center of the turn-around driveway. As the Jeep came around to the front of the cabin, she could see Marge's face peeping through the curtain, parted slightly with her hand. The look on Marge's face was similar to the look she'd displayed last evening. Again, Pat felt the cold, threatening stare to the very bottom of her soul, and wondered how long she would remain safe with Marge. She drove the Jeep down the long, tree-lined driveway. Through the rear-view mirror, she kept an observant eye on the cabin's front door.

———

William told his supervisor on Thursday that he would leave early Friday because of personal business that needed his attention, never mentioning that the true reason was the dance on Friday night. It had been a while since he'd been to one, and he remembered the fun he'd had with the out-of-town girls, the ones that were not from the area. *"Tonight will be a night to remember,"* he thought as he walked toward the power switch that lit every light in the series of fluorescents on the ceiling.

As he returned toward the checkout area and heard the customer entrance door open and close behind the approaching footsteps, he thought, *"Christ, I was hoping this would be an easy day."* As he rounded the corner, the sight of trooper Harry Circus in all his polished glory surprised him. "Good morning, Harry. You're out early this morning."

"Busy, busy!" Harry said. "Is your boss around, William? I'd like to ask him a couple of questions."

"Nope, I'm the only one here this morning, Harry."

"Well, maybe you can help me."

"If I can, Harry, you know I'll always help the law if I can, that's what I always say." Harry stared at William with a kind of disbelieving "you've got to be kidding me" look.

"Great, we need a lot more people like you. Now let me ask you this, have there been more sales than normal with your 30/30 ammo?"

"Well, come to think of it, I think so. Come over here and let's have a look. I restocked the shelves just a few days ago, and I'd know how much was sold. I don't work evenings so I don't know what anyone else has sold. I only know what I've sold."

"That's fine, William; you just tell me how much has been sold since you last stocked the shelves. OK?"

"Sure, Harry, I can do that, no problem." They walked through the sporting-goods section, and Harry glanced at the new rods and reels standing neatly on the racks. He was thinking to himself as they walked how much he'd like to have one of those babies, and a whole month off next summer. *"I sure would like to get away for a while,"* he thought.

"Here we are, Harry, let's see now, right hea', 30/30. I put twelve boxes up theya' the day that retard jumped me."

"What?" Harry asked.

"You know that retard theya, Marge, from town? I was going to call you, but Pat kind of talked me out of it theya'. She said that I shouldn't have called Marge a retard. She was probably right, I guess, she just ticks me off is all."

"Tell me what happened!" Harry demanded, and William more than willingly relayed the events in the store that morning. When he finished, Harry asked, "Why were they here?"

"Now that you mention it, Harry, she asked me for some 30/30's, but after all the shit that went down, they left without 'em."

Harry now looked up at the shelf. "Tell me, William, how many boxes were sold since you restocked?"

"Looks like five boxes gone, but I didn't sell 'em, Harry."

"Is that an unreasonable amount to have sold this time of year?"

"Not really, but we have been selling a lot of 30/30's lately."

"Thanks, William. I'll be checking with you later."

"Anytime, Harry, always like to help the law."

Harry smiled but said nothing as he walked toward the door.

—

Lester entered the bank at exactly one minute after nine. Darcy greeted him with a smug sort of smile, making him feel uneasy, and forcing him to recall the events of a few days earlier when he'd reached for her knee. *"I'll get her for this,"* he thought.

"Good morning, Lester." Irene offered him a sunny smile.

"Good morning, Irene. Would you come into my office when you get a moment, please?" Looking around, Irene gave her favorite prissy look to the other tellers. "I'll be right in, Lester."

Darcy wanted to throw up. "Oh, I'd like to plant my foot on her big ass," she whispered softly to herself. After Irene had reported to Lester, he informed the other tellers they were not to be disturbed except for an emergency. A couple of the younger tellers laughed softly after hearing Darcy's comment, "Old Lester the lecher."

Lester's hands were roaming freely over Irene's entire body as she stood by his desk chair. "I was thinking that you and I could probably make that dance tonight, if you're free." It was not his intention to take her to the dance; after all…Lester was a married man. It just sounded better to tell her that. If they did go, he would most likely meet her there.

"Oh, I'm free, Lester," Irene said.

"You know what I like to do after dancing?" Lester grinned out the question.

"No, tell me, Lester, what do you like to do after dancing?"

"Come with me, my little cutie," he said, and taking her by the hand, he led her into his file closet and closed the door.

From her teller's window, Darcy thought she could hear an occasional bumping sound coming from Lester's back room, but dismissed it as the sounds coming from the drive-up window's speaker.

—

When Pat pulled into the Quick-Stop parking lot, Jimmy's pickup was nowhere in sight. *"I hope I haven't missed him,"* she thought, then parked the Jeep and went inside. She greeted several of the regular customers; then took a seat at the last table near the window. That way she could see every vehicle that came and went from the parking lot. She was about to sip her coffee when her heart thumped at the sound of Jimmy's approaching pickup. *"Oh yes,"* she thought, *"no Marge around this time,"* and realized that she was smiling.

So was Jimmy as he walked in. "Hello there, Pat, You look bright and cheerful as usual, beautiful too."

Pat could feel a blush come over her face, and all that came out was, "No sir."

Jimmy sat across from her at the table. They stared into one another's eyes for what seemed to be the longest time. As far as they were concerned, they were the only ones in the place. Finally Jimmy broke the silence. "How'd you two make out yesterday—out to camp, I mean?"

"Out to camp?" Pat asked.

"Yeah, didn't you tell me you and Marge were going out to camp yesterday?"

"Oh, right, we did, not much going on out there." She'd forgotten their conversation at Walter's.

"You know, Pat, tonight is the dance over at the VFW, and I… I was wondering if you, ah, might want to…ah, go?" Pat thought he'd never get it out.

"To the dance…with you? Sure, I'd love to. Will you pick me up?"

"You bet I will." Jimmy's voice was trembling. "I'll pick you up at around 7:30. Would that be all right with you?"

"Fine, see you then." Pat wanted to stay with him, but she didn't want Marge to think she wasn't coming back and come looking for her. She explained that to Jimmy, and they said their good-byes.

—

Marge had long since finished her breakfast, and the fishing gear was ready to go. Their idea of fishing was far different from the "sports" up on the river that fished for salmon with their expensive fly-casting equipment. This time of year, in late summer, several species of fish were migrating back to the sea. Pat and Marge loved to catch them with dip nets and spears, but their favorite catch was eel. They did not believe in hunting or fishing licenses—those were for the sports, the ones with the big money.

Marge was becoming impatient, and went for her 30/30 to target-shoot while waiting for Pat's return. "Little Pat bitch, little Pat bitch, left me alone again." She loaded the rifle with as many rounds as it could hold, and began firing at the artificially stuffed deer they'd placed about fifty yards into a thicket behind the cabin. There was no question about Marge's ability with a rifle. Each shot was placed exactly where she aimed—she knew that by the puffs of material lifted from the stuffed deer with the impact of each bullet.

Marge started to chant now with each shot. "Come home now, Pat." Boom! "Come home now, Pat." Boom! From the far end of the driveway, Pat heard the shots and stopped the Jeep, locking the wheels. The sound of shooting itself wasn't a big deal. They both target-shot often here. Things were a bit different this morning, however. Pat waited, and proceeded forward when the shooting stopped, assuming Marge was reloading. As she drove toward the house, she wondered how Marge would react when she told her about going to the dance alone with Jimmy tonight.

—

At that very moment, across town, Davis Norton had only one thing on his mind...going out to his camp. His pickup had been loaded since the evening before, and all that was left was to choose the right rod and reel, and a rifle. He always said that a person should be prepared for anything when they go out to camp, and in a few short minutes, he would be on his way. An avid gun collector, he always seemed to know from the many guns in his collection exactly which one he would choose at any given time. Shortly after he entered the house, he exited with a 30/30 in his left hand, and the tube containing a rod and reel tucked tightly under his arm, convinced he was leaving this world behind for two full days and two full nights of undisturbed quiet.

—

Marge was about to reload when she heard the Jeep approaching, and lowered the rifle. The Jeep rumbled to a stop, and before calm restored itself to the area, Marge began her verbal assault on Pat.

"So, little Pat bitch, you said you'd be back before I finished my breakfast, and

I've been finished a long time now."

"I know," Pat said. "I had to wait for Jimmy—he was late, and it turned out that we had a little more to talk about than I thought."

"Oh sure, little Pat, I'm sure it was that."

Pat immediately suggested they check an eel trap. This would hopefully allow Marge time to cool down before telling her of her plans with Jimmy. "I could go for a couple of them this weekend," Marge said excitedly. "I've got the dip net, boots, and the buckets right over there," she said as she pointed toward the woodpile.

"Great, let's head down there and see how many we've got."

Marge moved toward the Jeep with her rifle in hand. "Wait!" Pat said quickly. "Why don't you leave it here this time? You won't have to shoot any eels, you know."

"Well, I guess I could," was Marge's response, and they loaded the gear into the Jeep, Marge brought the rifle into the house and then they left.

As they approached the final curve in the driveway, they noticed that the entire way was blocked with Harry Circus' official car, its rear antennas whipping as it stopped suddenly at the very edge of the drive. Harry immediately got out, stood by the hood of his trooper car, and waited for the Jeep to arrive.

"Good morning, ladies…where are we off to today?" His probing, curious eyes searched the vehicle. Both women remained silent, staring at the trooper. "I wanted to ask Marge a couple of questions."

"I didn't do nothin," Marge replied.

"Well, now, I didn't say you did, did I?" Marge just stared directly into Harry's eyes, with her chin tucked toward her chest. "I'd like to know what happened between you and William at the variety store the other day."

"He called me a retard, you know."

When Pat heard Marge's reply, she got out of the Jeep. "Harry!" He interrupted her.

"I'd like her to answer me, Pat, if you don't mind." She wondered why he had to pass himself off as such a major pain in the ass.

He turned back to Marge. "Well, Marge, can you help me with that?"

"What do you want?" Marge asked, now seemingly confused and disoriented.

"I asked if you could tell me what happened between you and William at the variety the other day."

"I told you…he called me a retard."

Pat started to say something, and Harry held up his hand, motioning her to be still.

"Then what happened after he called you that?" Marge was frowning, looking down as if being scolded by a disciplining parent. Almost inaudibly, Marge responded with, "I jumped on him."

"Were you trying to hurt him, Marge?"

"He called me a retard, I told you." The words came a little louder this time.

Harry looked to Pat. "Is that the way it went down?"

"Yah, Harry that's it." She was angry at the way Harry had questioned Marge, but voicing her opinion now would only make matters worse.

Harry motioned for Pat to follow him as he walked toward the trooper car, and as they arrived at the driver's door, Harry spoke. "Look, Pat, I know what you're up against with her. I've been hearing things about Marge. It sounds like she's out of control. Correct me if I'm wrong, but I don't think I am. William told me that she's been buying a lot of 30/30 ammo. Is that true?"

"We buy our share. Why, is there a law against target shootin', Harry?"

"You know better than that, Pat, and you also know that there are laws against night hunting, and shooting road signs."

"Are you accusing us of something, Harry? Because if you are..."

"You hold it right there. Pat, if I were going to accuse you of anything, I'd be down here with the facts. Like I said before, I've heard some things and I'm only asking some questions, that's all. Now you tell her to watch her step, because I'll be watching." Harry got into the car, which he had left running, and pulled away quickly, leaving Pat somewhat numb with anger. She could write a book on the way she felt about Harry Circus right now, but the only word that would come as she watched the speeding car pull away was, "Asshole!"

—

Davis Norton was many miles from town, entering the vast forest that he so unequivocally loved. The narrow road was wide enough for one vehicle. It had been years since he'd ventured out to this particular place. He turned his mind to how he would find it. Speaking aloud to himself as he drove, he said, "Well I hope this old place hasn't been broken into, and everything stolen. Wouldn't surprise me none though, the way people are now-a-days. Can't trust nobody."

His mind ushered him back to the wonderful times spent at the camp. Solitude would be his again. The pickup wound its way through the thick encompassing forest, over and down steep rough hills that led to shallow rock-bound, babbling brooks easily negotiated by the big, four-wheel drive vehicle. Davis pictured in his mind the cabin nestled deep beneath the giant pines and scattered hardwoods, and he longed for this tranquility that he was sure lay no more than a mile ahead of him.

Nothing, however, could have prepared him for what he was to find. The pickup strained somewhat as it ascended the steepness of the final hill to the summit, which would reveal the cabin and its glorious surroundings. As the vehicle crested the top of the hill, Davis's scream of pain could have been heard for a mile in any direction, had there been ears to hear it. The look on his face was comparable to someone waking to find the remains of a loving pet that passed away during the night. There, before him, his beloved cabin stood tall and strong in the middle of a clear-cut. Nothing was left of the forest except for a few deformed and skeletal remains of what once were trees.

Stunned into emotional paralysis, Davis mumbled, yet nothing seemed audible even to himself. Thoughts of yesterday flashed before him, only to vanish as quickly as they appeared. His mind searched itself for answers, but none surfaced except an almost-forgotten story he had read long ago, something he believed would never happen here.

*"Continuing on your way, you have in your mind a picture developed long ago of every turn and bend in the road, yet for some strange reason you feel totally unfamiliar with the entire area. There are roads now where not a road lay before; survey lines and flagging are a continuous mark on the forest. You search your memory for landmarks, and you remember the road that would bring you to your special place would be marked by the very large boulder, yet you have not passed such a landmark and you continue on your course. Suddenly you enter a very large unfamiliar clearing with a similar-looking boulder to the south of the road. Your mind filled with anguish, you are frustrated beyond belief. There is absolutely no forest here any longer. These surroundings were unfamiliar because there is nothing left here but a barren section of land that was once your vast, green forest, a place in which you once felt such solitude amongst such life. You stop your vehicle and step out, realizing that you are but a short way from what once was the squirrel's tree. Looking all about you in every direction, you now observe a vast barren land of nothingness. All that remains are the twisted, deformed hulks of what were majestic hardwoods. You can go no farther in search of the squirrel's tree, for as far as the eye can see, there is nothing..."*

## CHAPTER 5

PAT RETURNED TO THE JEEP after losing sight of the trooper's car on its way back to town. What she saw upon climbing into the Jeep was a shaken and totally withdrawn Marge.

She spoke gently. "Are you all right, Marge?"

"He didn't have to talk to me like that, Pat, did he, did he?"

"No, he didn't. He really pissed me off. Look, why don't we go check the eel trap anyway? I'm sure he won't bother us any more today."

"Maybe we could, little Pat, maybe we could." Pat felt melancholic over the whole situation as she started the Jeep and began to drive. Marge was incredibly quiet as she sat in her usual back-seat location, staring out of the open rear window, focused on nothing in particular. Pat wondered how she could possibly ask her to stay alone tonight while she and Jimmy went to the dance. Glancing at Marge through the rear-view mirror, she tried to dismiss the thought as she turned the Jeep onto an old skidder road left uneven, with enough exposed stone to make it almost impassable.

"That trooper won't follow us down here, will he, Pat, not down here?"

"I think you may have something there, Marge." As the next couple of hours passed, Marge seemed to take hold of herself, displaying the bizarre antics of her usual demeanor. Somewhat relieved, Pat thought the time right to field a few questions about tonight. "Marge, how are you doing over there?"

"I'm good, little Pat, good! Did you see the size of this eel?" Holding up the large dip net and revealing an eel of a length and thickness that would make some men shiver with dread, she said with a huge grin, "I can't remember when we got one this big." A few moments passed as they examined the large specimen, then Pat thought the time right. "Marge, remember this morning when I went to meet with Jimmy?"

"Yes, I do, little Pat!"

"Well, he asked me if I would go with him tonight, ah…to a dance."

"We're goin' to a dance, goin' to a dance." Marge sang.

"Well, I think we should talk about that. I was hoping you might consider staying home to keep the fire burning, maybe clean this big eel, it sure would be a big help to me."

"Oh, sure. You stay home, Marge, you stay home!" Marge's anger spewed. What Pat expected now was a knockdown, drag-out battle, but to her amazement, Marge's attitude changed as quickly as a light being switched on. "I'm sorry, little Pat, you should go. I've got plenty to do cleaning this big eel. I might cut a piece and eat it, and you'll have to wait 'til tomorrow."

—

Pat was frozen to the spot. At any moment, she half-expected Marge to latch onto the large eel, swing it over her head, and wrap it around Pat's neck. "What did you say, Marge?"

"I said you should go, it would do you good."

"That's what I thought you said." Pat shook her head and looked back over her shoulder with every second or third step she took heading out, away from the water. "Are you sure you're all right, Marge?"

"Look, little Pat, you want me to change my mind?"

"Oh, no! That's fine, Marge, please don't change your mind, I'll go." Pat wondered if the incident with Harry a short while ago might have messed Marge up. She would certainly keep an eye on her for the next couple of hours before leaving for the dance.

—

Lester spent all of Friday boasting to anyone who would listen. He would be attending the VFW dance this evening, but he left out one important part: he would be meeting his favorite teller, Irene. Lester's wife, Betty, would be out of town for the weekend, leaving good old Lester a free bird. Irene spent the day popping from teller station to telephone, telephone to drive-up window, and back into Lester's office. Watching the two of them reminded Darcy of a couple of cooing pigeons leaving their droppings all over someone's roof. All in all, the day went by rather quickly. Lester was leaving early anyway, which made it even better.

Darcy whispered to another teller, "If we can only get rid of that fat, little hen there, we'll finish Friday rather nicely." On Fridays, the bank normally closed at six o'clock. At three o'clock, Lester wished everyone a good weekend, winked at Irene, and left. Irene knew that she was to go straight home when the bank closed at six, and wait for Lester's call. He would make that call after his wife left. The three hours that remained of the afternoon were passing intolerably slow for Irene, making her more irritable. With each passing minute, she became more consciously jealous of the fact that while she, Lester's favorite teller, sat minding the bank, Lester was at home alone with his wife. What Irene could not know while this thought was crossing the depths of her mind, was that Lester's wife was informing him that she would not be leaving for the weekend, as previously planned.

—

"What do you mean, my dear?" was Lester's hoarse and confused response.

"Yes, Lester, I know how much you love to dance, and for the last several months, I've not given you much of my time. Lester, my dear, you and I will dance the night away at the VFW tonight! Are you surprised, my dear?"

"Oh…am I surprised!" was all that Lester was able to mutter.

—

Harry Circus was on the phone with Ralph Bailey, Berryville's constable. Ralph's voice burbled through the receiver. "Harry, were you planning to make an appearance at the dance tonight?"

"Not if I can help it," was Harry's response.

"I wanted to check with you to make sure," Ralph said.

"Trouble never happens at those dances, and besides, I'm planning to take the whole weekend for things I've been putting off here, at the house." Harry said.

"Will you be at home tonight just in case I need to call you for anything?"

"Oh sure, Ralph. Annie and I were going to get a couple of movies and hang out here, so if you need something, just make sure it's important, Ralph."

"No problem, Harry. Have a good weekend, and I hope I don't see ya."

"Me, too," Harry said and hung up. He turned to his notes from the week, making sure that anyone he needed to contact had been crossed off the list. He couldn't help wondering when his eyes fell on the final entry in his book…*"MARGE"*, he thought to himself, *"Now, that is a woman out of control. She is going to become a problem and I'll have to keep tabs on this one."* He closed his book, hoping it would remain closed for the weekend.

—

At 7:00 p.m., Irene sat furiously by the phone that hadn't rung. She was breathing heavily, and her entire body trembled with anger. "Where is that little bastard?" She cried. "I knew it! I shouldn't have let him talk me into staying at the bank. Any one of those little tramp tellers could have closed the bank." Finally, she couldn't take it any longer. She got her coat and went out to her car. *"I have to find out what happened. There must be a reason why he didn't call,"* was her thought as she started her car and backed out of the driveway.

She drove past the VFW, but it was too early. There were only a few cars there. "Calm down," she said aloud, "there must be a reasonable explanation why he didn't call." She now thought back to the day in the bank. *"I know he cares for me, because of the way we hold each other in his office, the way we touch. I don't care… I'm going to drive by his house. I have to see what's going on."*

Once she got on Main Street, it would be a short drive to the circular, heavily tree-lined lane where Lester lived. It was a very dark road to begin with, and now that night was near, Irene felt confident her slow approach to the house would not be detected.

43

She turned onto the lane road and slowed the vehicle to a crawl. As she passed the large Victorian on the left, Irene could see the lights from Lester's house. As the house became more visible, she slowed the vehicle to a point that it crawled forward under its own weight. With her headlights off, she dared not tap the brake pedal so as not to reveal her presence as the vehicle passed.

Because the windows were closed, the scream that came from within the vehicle could not be heard outside. Tears immediately began to flow freely down Irene's cheeks. Her jealousy was matched only by the anger that overtook every cell of her being. Through the side of the large picture window, Irene could see Lester and Betty locked in a passionate embrace.

—

The sun appeared as a massive blazing planet capable of scorching the earth itself on its approach to sunset. Davis Norton, feeling total emptiness within, slowed his vehicle for lack of vision from the setting sun, glaring through the windshield at eye level. Nothing seemed the same any longer. His mind, wanted to transport him to the past. Davis's movements—even the simplest of actions—were mechanical, as his instincts came into play. He reached for the bottle of booze he'd brought, drinking deeply to ease the pain.

He headed back toward town, talking aloud to steady his thoughts. "Why would anyone in their right mind cut all those trees near the camp like that? I've never seen anything like it—not a single tree left. Gone, totally gone. The camp looks stupid sitting out in the open like that." As each thought passed his lips, his foot pressed harder on the accelerator, and the heavy vehicle began a high-speed descent down the long steep grade that wound its way to the thickly settled community below. Davis, holding the wheel tightly with his left hand, threw the empty whiskey bottle out the window. Hearing it smash on the pavement behind him forced him to laugh uncontrollably; while his only thought now was to get more Jack Daniels.

———

After arriving back at the house, Marge was acting somewhat nervous and very preoccupied with her thoughts. Pat's mind was on one thing and one person: the dance tonight and Jimmy White. In a few short hours, Jimmy would be picking her up for an evening she hoped neither of them would forget for a long time. Marge had wasted no time cleaning and skinning the large eel that they'd brought back with them. She wrapped it in foil and after placing it into the fridge, turned quickly and called out to Pat. "I think I'm going to take a walk into town."

Pat seemed a little surprised, but welcomed the thought of being alone to enjoy the hot waters of her bath. "Why do you want to walk to town, Marge?"

"No reason. I just want to get out by myself for a while, that's all."

"Well, no problem. Do you think you'll be back before I leave for the dance?"

"Not sure, little Pat, not sure."

"Well, okay, Marge, if I don't see you before I leave, I'll see you when I get home." As Pat prepared her bath, she wondered at how odd the relationship between herself and Marge had become. Apart from being sort of a guardian, at times she felt more like a worrisome parent with a growing teenager that was now becoming more and more a burden to her social life. "Ha! What social life?" Pat laughed while lowering herself into the hot, soothing bath water. There was however, the secret she had promised to keep.

—

Lester jumped, and almost pushed Betty off balance when he heard the roar of the speeding car's engine as it pulled away from the front of his home. He glanced quickly through the large picture window to see the lights of a vehicle being turned on as it disappeared quickly in the thickening growth of trees and the rapidly encroaching darkness. Betty blinked and asked, "What was that all about, Lester?"

"Oh, you know my dear, it's Friday night—probably some overzealous school kid wasting gasoline." But Lester kept his back toward her so as not to reveal his bulging eyes and a look on his face that he was certain would not be explainable. He knew that Irene had just seen him and his wife holding each other, and could only imagine the pain she must have felt. *"Oh shit!"* he thought to himself. *"What must she be thinking?"* Then, the most horrible thought entered his mind. *"After all this, would Irene be daring enough, angry enough to show up at the dance tonight anyway and make a scene?"*

Lester wanted to be alone to think this all out, but darling Betty would have none of it. "Lester darling, I'm warm all over for you. Come to me, Lester." His stomach was in knots. How could he think of sex with her now when the woman he really wanted to be with was driving away through the night in a speeding car?

"Betty, please. I'm sorry, I'd forgotten that I was supposed to call and see that everything tallied right at the bank this afternoon."

"Oh, come now, Lester, those girls don't need you to close that bank. Now you come right here to me and let me warm those cute little buns of yours."

—

Constable Bailey arrived at the VFW hall at 7:15 p.m. The usual set-up people were there, making sure the freezers were well stocked with ice, and all the cases of soft drinks brought in from the locked shed out back. Ralph helped a couple of older women retie some ticker-tape decorations on the building's support beams, and good old anxious William had arrived, bug-eyed and drooling on anything that could be considered an available young lady.

The VFW's policy for events such as a dance like this one was B.Y.O.B. That left the door open for a variety of situations to develop, requiring the presence of a local constable. When the early arrivals started to trickle in, Ralph looked at his watch. It was 7:45 p.m. He noticed a longhaired young man walk in through the stage door carrying a guitar in one hand and a microphone in the other. He was followed by two more longhaired young men and several spaced-out-looking young women wearing black leather jackets and carrying two base drums.

"Oh, shit!" Ralph said in an almost inaudible tone. "Goddamned Rock-and-Rollers. Probably smokin' pot and drinkin' whiskey. Shit! There's gonna be trouble tonight. Goddammit, I knew it."

## CHAPTER 6

---

THE LOCAL AND OUT-OF-TOWN CROWD began trickling into the
VFW hall, and the parking lots in front and to the side were
beginning to fill. Several vehicles were parked in the road—those
probably belonging to the older people who planned to leave early
and could do so easily by parking out there. The band could be
heard a quarter of a mile away, as they had tied into the hall's PA
system.

After several warm-up numbers, Eddie, who lived behind the
VFW and who was always on hand to clean up after a party, was
asked by a couple of older partygoers if he could get the band to
tone it down a notch. After a couple of dirty looks from the band
members, the amps were turned down, but never enough for the
older crowd. Several couples on the dance floor signaled their
displeasure, and the band reciprocated by turning up the volume.

In the far corner, two tables were pulled together to accommodate
a larger crowd. Three couples dressed in black leather jackets and
motorcycle boots had claimed the area. The empty whiskey bottles

began to clink in the corner. On top of the table, the empty beer cans were stacked neatly in a wall-like construction. Ralph Bailey had positioned himself next to the wall-mounted pay phone across the room, and he began to wonder if the bikers would be the beginning of the evening's trouble, keeping in mind what Harry had said earlier: "Make sure it's important."

"I just wish he were here." Ralph whispered to himself.

As much as Jimmy wanted to be with Pat, he could not stop his stomach from fluttering as he drove up her driveway. From inside, Pat could hear the vehicle approaching, and went to a window, parting the curtain slightly. Upon recognizing Jimmy's vehicle, she began smiling like a schoolgirl flirting with a boy. She waited until she heard the motor stop, then went to the door to greet him. As the door swung open, their eyes locked, and neither one of them could speak. Jimmy moved forward, his eyes moving slowly over her lovely face, studying the fullness of her lips. Simultaneously they closed their eyes and met in a warm, deep kiss.

It seemed both had waited their lifetimes for this very moment, and neither of them wanted it to end, nor be the first to try to move away. After several moments, Jimmy made the first move and said, "Hello."

Pat smiled and said, "Hello," and they went inside. They still seemed entranced with each other, but now more willing to chat and share in their excitement of being together.

"Pat, you look great!" Jimmy said. She was wearing a new pair of black jeans that fit her contour snugly, held at the waist with a wide black leather belt and gold buckle. Her pink blouse had two top buttons open, and she had on a pair of well-polished black western boots. Her long black hair, held back with a pink ribbon, gave her a very country-girl, very feminine look. It was as if the two of them had collaborated on how they would dress, minus the pink blouse and ribbon, Jimmy's clothes were identical, except for his navy blue western shirt.

After a few moments of exchanging compliments and small talk, Jimmy noticed that the usual second pair of eyes which generally accompanied Pat weren't present. "Where is Miss Marge tonight?" Jimmy asked.

"Well, she left about an hour ago. I thought she would have come back by now. She told me she was walking to town because she wanted to be alone for a while. I'm a little worried."

"That's funny," Jimmy remarked. "I came through town. I never saw her."

Pat seemed to be a million miles away in thought, and then realizing she was not alone, said, "I'm sorry Jimmy; I'm getting so wrapped up in her lately. There doesn't seem to be time for much else."

"I'll be working on that tonight if you let me," and with that said, Pat reached for her sweater on the chair, and they turned toward the door. She made a final glance around the cabin. Her last thought as she closed the door behind herself was of Marge, and she hoped she would be all right.

The reason that Jimmy never saw Marge as he passed through town was that Marge had walked along the riverbank, as her intention was to be alone. She needed time by herself to let her mind wander back to when she had felt good about life. Marge had dressed herself for the cool evening. Over her usual T-shirt, she wore a red and black check logger's flannel over which she had pulled on an insulated, hooded sweatshirt with a pouch pocket on the front. In the pouch, she carried a warm pair of gloves and her flashlight. On her head was a red and black checked visor cap, the type with earmuffs folded inside if needed. The legs of her bibbed jeans were stuffed into her calf-high rubber boots. Hanging from her belt was a black leather sheath that housed her favorite hunting knife.

Marge never went anywhere without her waterproof matches, her pipe with tobacco pouch, and God forbid, at least one can of Bud stuffed tightly in the large rear pocket of her trousers. All that remained of daylight now was a thin orange line enhancing the shadows of distant mountains. Marge sat herself on the cut of a large stump, stuffed her bowl with tobacco, popped the top on the beer and settled back to enjoy what little time she had to be alone.

Before her pipe became completely lit, her thoughts returned as they always did to Harvey and their many cherished experiences together—their hunting and fishing trips, and the quiet time when there weren't many people around. "I miss you, Harvey," she said softly, then she began speaking to herself. "You know, I still love huntin' and fishin', and Pat does, too. We do good things together. Sometimes I think she doesn't want me around, but she does, she does! Next time I go huntin', I'm gonna kill somethin' big, kill somethin' big."

Suddenly, out of nowhere, Marge's attitude changed again. "I'd like to kill that goddamned cop Harry. Yeah, kill Harry. He didn't have to treat me like that. He thinks I'm a retard like everyone else, but I'm not a retard." Marge guzzled the rest of her beer, pitching the can onto a flat rock and flattening it with her foot while repeating in a chant-like verse with each stomping of her heel. "I hate that fuckin' Harry, hate that fuckin' Harry!"

—

Irene was wearing the same clothes she had worn when leaving for the bank this morning. Observing Lester and his wife had left her numb and considerably dazed. She had always believed everything Lester said concerning the two of them, and he had left her little doubt that he would eventually leave his wife. Her feelings for him were unmistakable. She wanted him.

She had to know, one way or another. What was going on between Lester and his wife? Why hadn't she kept her plans to be out of town for the weekend? This should have been their time! The thought of seeing them together ran through her mind repeatedly. For the last hour, Irene had driven the narrow, winding roads that led from one small town to another. It was now approaching 8:00 p.m. She had not eaten since noon. Combining that with her present state of mind and fatigue, it was impossible for her to think clearly or to continue driving much longer. She made a decision. Grasping the steering wheel tightly, she turned the vehicle around and drove toward Berryville.

Upon arriving in town, she began to feel a deep uneasiness come over her, wondering what exactly she would do if she saw Betty and Lester. *"Will I make a scene?"* was her first thought. *"Betty supposedly knows nothing about us. Maybe it's all just a crazy mistake. Stay cool; don't do anything stupid,"* she tried to reassure herself. Suddenly Lester's vehicle appeared in the distance. Turning at the Route 1 intersection, it became illuminated by the lights at the corner. Irene, keeping at a distance, followed it in the direction of the VFW hall. It was 8:30 p.m. The next few minutes took forever to go by for Irene as she followed and waited to see where Lester would go.

Lester drove into the VFW lot. It looked as if he was having trouble deciding whether or not to stop the vehicle or to continue on his way. Irene strained her vision so that she might observe the passengers and exactly what they would do. She could see from his movements that Lester was nervous. He kept turning his head in all directions as if he were expecting someone to come from behind at any moment. *"He wants to look out!"* Irene breathed from her silent post.

The vehicle pulled ahead slowly to an available parking space about fifty yards away from the entrance of the hall. A moment passed, and both driver and passenger doors opened simultaneously. Lester got out first. Irene felt her heart sink deep within her as she recognized the red pullover sweater that Lester was wearing as the one she give him last Christmas. She breathed shallowly as the gentlemanly Lester went to assist his wife from the vehicle, closing the door behind her. "You never opened the door for me like that," Irene uttered in a groan. It was all she could do to remain where she was watching them walking, their arms around each other, toward an evening meant for her and Lester. Feeling more alone than she had ever felt in her life, she watched as Lester turned to give one final glance into the darkness, then the large door of the hall swung closed behind them.

—

It was obvious to everyone who saw Davis Norton walk into the dance that he was totally smashed. His speech was slurred; he tripped on everything. Watching him from what had become his secure perch by the wall phone; Ralph Bailey studied Davis's slow, unsteady approach to the corner of the hall, already taken over by the biker's group, now doubled in size. Davis, looking as though he had just arrived from army camp, wore a full camouflage outfit, including his boots, and a hunting knife with camouflage handle and sheath. The only article of clothing that looked out of place was the white webbed belt with a brass cinch buckle that he wore around his waist.

He was still at a considerable distance from the bikers, yet he seemed to be looking in their general direction, swinging his half-drunk bottle of Jack Daniels in a toasting motion as if inviting the bikers and their women to drink with him. When he was still several tables away, Davis was noticed by several of the bikers, who immediately began urging him to come share his bottle, and from the look on his face, he was more than willing.

William Bradley, who had been watching Davis since he'd walked in, charged out from between two tables and deliberately rammed into Davis, knocking him to the floor and breaking the bottle. The bikers instantly became a loud, disapproving mob.

"Shit," was all Ralph Bailey could say as he moved quickly through the crowd on the dance floor, many of whom hadn't noticed anything.

"I saw that, William!" he hollered. "What the hell did you do that for?"

"I didn't do anything. That shithead's drunk and you know it." Davis, who had now latched onto a chair, was trying without success to right himself and face his assailant. Ralph had positioned himself between the two, glaring at William, and did not see Davis reaching around him to get at the young man. The grab, deflected by a punch to Davis's forearm by William, knocked him quickly off balance. Ralph's eager attempt to prevent Davis from falling again was in vain. The wind and the fight now completely knocked out of him, Davis remained on the floor. "I ought to run you in for that, William. You could have hurt him real bad."

"Shit, he's so drunk I could a' killed that retard and he'd never a' felt anything."

"You better get out of my sight right now or I'll call Harry and have him take care of you." William mumbled something and gave Ralph a dirty look, then walked away. "Come on Davis, let's get you off the floor." Ralph reached under each armpit and lifted old Davis to his feet. "Are you hurt?"

"No, I'm not hurt, you leave me alone, and I'll be fine." Ralph assisted him to a table and eased him down onto a chair.

Ralph spoke clearly so Davis would understand in his drunken fog. "I'd appreciate it if you'd stay here until I get back." Davis did not respond. Ralph went to the kitchen for coffee, but when he returned, Davis was gone.

—

The evening continued on with no sign of further trouble. That alone gave Ralph Bailey much satisfaction. William had gone from one rejection to another, until finally finding what appeared to be the girl of his dreams. Ralph watched them for a few moments as they nestled in a corner. He noticed that had her hair been cut and shaped differently, the two could have been mistaken for twins. Both were thin and gaunt, while each displayed a long and dainty nose, bent now under the pressure of a kiss. Ralph shook his head with a look of disgust, and turned away to scrutinize the bikers' behavior. Several of the men, using their arms as pillows, were stretched out over the table, and two of the women were being fondled by one of the large, bearded and still conscious black-leathered bikers. He hoped that none of the older partygoers would complain so that the evening would end troubled only by the Davis and William disturbance. He couldn't help wonder however, where Davis had gone.

—

Lester and Betty danced from the time they arrived, and continued to dance after many couples had retired to their tables and their drinks. Lester, in his red pullover sweater, gray chinos, and soft black leather chukka boots, looked an amiable partner for Betty, in her black button-up sweater with gold buttons, matching double-knit pants, and black slipper-like shoes. Ralph snickered to himself as the shining, nearly bald top of Lester's head glistened under the lights from the stage. The band had finally given in to requests for slower tunes, and was playing "The Sea of Love" for the only two people on the dance floor, Lester and Betty.

"Ah, this was no big deal at all," Ralph said, breathing a sigh of relief. "Harry will be proud. The local lawman keeps the peace again. Ah yes, this job gets easier every day," he said, while heading toward the kitchen and a final cup of coffee.

—

The evening flew by. For the first time in years, Lester had felt an unusually warm calmness between Betty and himself. Except for the occasional need to look over his shoulder for fear that Irene might storm in and make an unwanted scene, he enjoyed his time here, and thought that Betty also enjoyed her time. As the small groups of friends started to leave, some people began closing up in the far corner of the hall, stacking chairs upon tables, preparing the hall to be cleaned.

"Well, my dear," Betty said. "I've had a wonderful evening."

"I, too, Betty, have had a wonderful evening." Lester smiled benignly at his wife.

"What shall we do now, handsome? I would think that most everything would be closed in the area at this time of night."

"Yes! I think you're right. Let's see…what if we return home and open a bottle of your favorite Merlot, play some soft music, and dance the night away?"

"Mmm…that sounds good, Lester, let's go." They left as they had arrived, arm in arm.

—

The evening had passed swiftly for yet another couple. Pat and Jimmy thoroughly enjoyed their time together. Although, neither was a good dancer, they had stayed out of the spotlight, finding their own little corner to talk and revel in each other's presence.

Pat was reluctant to leave. "I've had a great time, Jimmy," she offered.

"So have I. I don't want it to end."

"Neither do I," Pat said.

"It doesn't have to end. Come back to my place, stay the night."

"You know I can't do that, Jimmy. I've never left Marge alone since Harvey died, and now, more than ever, she needs me."

"What do you mean? Pat, for Christ's sake, she's a big girl now, and you don't have to baby-sit anymore."

"It's not that, it's just...well, she's been acting a little strange lately."

"Lately? She's been acting strange all of her damned life, you know that."

"Listen," Pat said. "Last week she jumped on William over there." They both looked toward William and his new love as they continued their kissing session in the corner.

"Whattaya mean, she jumped on him?"

"Just what I said. We went into to the variety to get some 30/30's. Marge kind of spooked William as a joke, then he jumped and called her a retard to her face. She freaked out and grabbed him. I thought she'd shake his head off. Harry was over this afternoon and gave her hell about it, and that kind of brought her down. She's not acting the same."

"So what!" Jimmy sputtered. "You'd act different for a while if Harry busted your butt."

"You don't understand, Jimmy. She's really acting different. I'm going to tell you something, and I don't want you to tell a soul, do you hear me?"

"I hear you, I'm not deaf," he snapped back.

"The other night, remember when we stopped to talk at

Walter's? Later that evening, we were heading back to town cross-country when we came upon Lennie's pickup. We stopped, and old Lennie was drunk, slumped over the wheel. I got out, seeing if he was all right, and when I get back in the Jeep I noticed that Marge had her freakin' rifle leveled at Lennie."

"You've gotta be shittin' me, Pat."

"No, so I asked her what the hell she was doing, and do you know what she said? 'I wonder what it would be like if I popped him in the head?'"

Jimmy sat frozen, staring at Pat for a moment before he asked, "What did you say after that?"

"I was scared. I don't remember exactly what I said, but I do remember telling her to leave her rifle in the back and come up front with me. At that point, I just didn't want her behind me."

"No shit, I know what you mean." Jimmy thought for a moment. "Have you told anyone else about this?"

"No, you're the only one." She was looking deep into his eyes now.

"I know you don't want me to tell anyone, but don't you think you're taking a hell of a chance with her? For Christ's sake, she could pop you anytime!"

"No, she wouldn't hurt me. Not Marge—we're too close. I'm all she has." Pat's thoughts were a million miles away, wondering if she really was safe with Marge right now.

Jimmy put his hands on Pat's arms. "I'm not going to feel very good knowing you're there with her, Pat. I never did trust her."

"I'll be fine. We really should think about getting back, though."

"Fine." Jimmy was unable to hide his displeasure, but said nothing further. They walked to the car in silence and got in. Jimmy drove slowly, wanting as much time with Pat as he could have because there was so little left to this evening. They talked about seeing each other on Sunday afternoon, and made small talk in the way that only lovers can do. They drove past the thick dark hulks of trees, and in the distance through the scattered thinning of jack fir, saw an occasional glimpse of the river.

Across the fields, dim lights showed through windows of distant farmhouses, though at this hour it was not customary to see anyone out and about. The evening emitted a feeling of simple serenity that both Pat and Jimmy had grown accustomed to in each other's presence, and welcomed.

They entered Pat's driveway, and Jimmy began talking rapidly, as if the words he now spoke would be his last. Pat motioned to him to stop the vehicle at the bottom of the driveway, and he did, but he kept talking. She placed her index finger over his lips, and when he stopped talking, she replaced the finger with her lips.

"Mmm..." was the only sound Jimmy could muster. After a short but very deep kiss, they again lost themselves in one another's eyes.

Several moments passed before Pat smiled and said, "Home, James."

"Yes, dear," he murmured, and again they pulled away, slowly making their way up the winding gravel driveway.

At the very first sight of the cabin, Pat knew something was wrong. There was no smoke coming from the chimney, and the cabin was dark. Even if Marge were home and had gone to bed, she would have loaded the stove, since there was quite a chill in the air.

"Oh, shit!" Pat said.

"What's wrong?" Jimmy asked.

"Marge isn't in there."

"How do you know that?"

"I know it, that's all." As soon as they stopped, Pat was out and walking quickly toward the house. "I should have known not to leave her." They went in to find the cabin cold. Marge had left before Jimmy arrived. She'd been gone for hours. "Where the hell could she be? It's after midnight."

"Could she be at someone's house, staying the night?" In spite of his dislike of Marge, he asked with concern.

"No, there's no place that she'd want to stay. Christ, I hope she hasn't gotten into trouble, or hurt herself." In a panic, Pat ran to see if Marge's 30/30 was where it always was.

—

When the phone rang, Lester and Betty had been sleeping quite soundly for about an hour with their arms locked around each other. Lester moaned slightly, grimacing as he reached for the receiver. "Yes, who is it?" The voice on the other end brought him wide awake immediately, as though a very loud alarm had gone off in his ear. He quickly turned to see if Betty was as conscious as he was, but the mixture of wine and dance were keeping her very much asleep.

"What do you want?" He asked at just above a whisper. Then, he remained silent as the caller continued speaking. Lester responded with, "No, that's impossible. I...I can't do that."

"Who is it, Lester?" Betty stirred beside him.

He had to think quickly. "It's...the sheriff's department, something about the bank's alarm system."

"Very good," the caller said, "now, I'll expect you in fifteen minutes behind the bank, and don't make me call this number again." The receiver was hammered down sharply in Lester's ear.

"What is it, Lester?"

"I'm going to have to go down to the bank, something about silencing the alarm."

"Not tonight!"

"Yes, I'm afraid so." Lester's voice was squeaking with nervousness. "You get some sleep, Betty. I'll be right back."

—

Harry was ushered out of a deep sleep by the incessant ring of the telephone. It began as the distant sound of a chime that would not be silenced. *"Somebody answer the phone,"* he thought. Suddenly wide awake, Harry lurched toward the ringing. Gasping, perspiring slightly, Harry moaned, "Hello!" Through the receiver, he could hear the sound of what seemed to be a crackling speaker or a bad connection, then a voice.

"Harry?"

"Yes, who is this?"

He could hear the strain in the caller's voice. "Harry, this is Ralph Bailey. I'm out here on the blueberry barrens."

"This better be good, Ralph, and what the hell time is it anyway?"

"3:10 a.m., Harry, and it's so good, I think I'm going to be sick." Through the telephone, Harry thought he could hear Ralph vomit, a deep heaving vomit.

"Ralph, what the hell's going on, where in hell are you?"

A moment later, Ralph's voice returned to the receiver. "Harry, I'm sorry. I'm just having a tough time with this. You'd better come out here as soon as you can. It's Lester Sawyer, the banker. He's dead. I mean he's fuckin' dead!"

"Where are you now, Ralph?"

"I'm calling you from my car. I'm out near the boat landing at Flynn Pond. It's pretty gross, Harry. Somebody really messed him up."

Harry spoke in a more subdued, considerate tone. He knew what Ralph was going through. "Am I going to have any trouble finding you?"

"No, you just head for the landing and you'll see me."

"I'm on my way." Harry placed the receiver down softly so he didn't wake Annie, but as he turned toward her, her eyes were as big as silver dollars.

"What was that all about?" she whispered.

"That was Ralph Bailey." Harry paused while looking into his wife's eyes. "He said they found Lester Sawyer's body out on the blueberry barrens."

"Oh God, what happened, Harry?" She strained to get up.

"I'll know more when I get out there. Can you fix me some coffee? I'll be leaving quickly."

"Sure, right away," she said and went directly downstairs. Harry dressed and had his car warming up before the coffee was fully perked. He quickly made a last minute check of his equipment, then jotted down notes of his verbal exchange with Ralph a few moments earlier, muttering to himself. "I can't believe it! Lester Sawyer, who in the hell would do this?"

"Now there's no need for you to drive fast, Harry. There's nothing you can do for him now. Getting yourself killed won't do any of us any good." When the words were out, Annie realized how foolish she must have sounded telling him that. Harry Circus never drove slowly. They kissed and exchanged I love you's. Harry, coffee cup in hand, went out the door. Annie watched the trooper car pull out of the drive, and become a blur upon entering the roadway as Harry sped away. Annie shook her head, smiled a half-smile. "Ha! Harry drive slow?" She returned to the kitchen for coffee, and what would probably be a long wait for her man.

—

As Harry approached Ridge Road, he decided that the highway north to the Hatchery Road would be quicker, so on came the lights, and the car zoomed off. The drive north was quick, no more than ten miles. On his way, he notified the police supervisor on duty that he was en route to a possible 1049 (the official term to signify a homicide), and gave him the location. From the tar to the landing was another four miles over gravel. The road was rough, with hundreds of potholes and thousands of protruding rocks embedded deep into the dirt, creating a rough and dusty ride.

While swerving the vehicle to avoid a large puddle in the center of the road as he neared the landing, his headlights focused on Ralph Bailey's town appropriated police car parked on the crest of a broad knoll. He could see Ralph leaning against the trunk, his chin tucked toward his chest. What Harry saw in front of the car no more than ten feet from the top of the knoll and illuminated by Ralph's headlights sent a shiver through his entire body. The blood-soaked, naked remains of Lester Sawyer had been tied to a makeshift wooden rack. He'd been disemboweled, and from his groin to his chest, he'd been partially skinned.

About twenty yards from Ralph's car on the edge of the field, Harry saw a pickup truck. He immediately recognized the truck, and the driver as Lennie, and wondered if he'd been the one to find Lester. Harry parked just over the crest of the knoll to conceal his vehicle and the scene from the soon-to-be passing outdoorsmen who frequented the area. Ralph appeared frozen to the spot. Even as Harry approached on foot, he could see that Ralph was visibly shaken.

Harry placed a hand on Ralph's shoulder and asked, "Are you all right?" The thought of finding his first body years before returned clearly and all too vividly to him. "Ralph, are you all right?" Harry repeated.

"Oh…yah. I'm fine now. I just never saw anything like this before. Kinda made me sick, you know?"

"I know. You stay here. I'll be right back," Harry said. What he'd seen in the past could not compare with the total gore that stood before him now. Lester Sawyer, who he'd known for years, had been brutally murdered. His eyes scanned the area around the murder scene, but for what, not even Harry was sure of. It was as if he were trying to delay the inevitable of having to examine the mutilated body of a person he'd known so well. He shook his head, and continued looking downward as if searching for something—anything that would delay the examination. "Dammit, there's nothing, not a damned thing here."

"Did you say something to me, Harry?" He heard Ralph's strained voice and looked toward him. The constable had not moved.

Harry said nothing. He advanced toward the gruesome remains, and took in every detail. "Oh, my God!" He had to force himself to look. "Why? How could anyone be sick enough to do something like this? I swear, I'll find the bastard if it takes the rest of my life," he said at just above a whisper. Harry stood before the remains, while thoughts of the past came to him in flashes. Lester was also an outdoorsman like himself. Fishing and hunting were a passion they shared. Suddenly, a vision of Lester knee-deep in the river came to him, his wet chest waders glistening in the sunlight. Harry had to move away, as the feeling of sickness nearly overcame him.

Harry walked back to his car, stopping first to see how Ralph was holding up. He knew what he was going through as the thoughts of witnessing his first murder scene kept coming back to him. Ralph's eyes focused on nothing, and he seemed lost on a distant thought. "Ralph, are you going to make it?" Harry tried to sound confident, but as the words came out, they sounded all wrong. Ralph made no effort to respond. "Is Lennie parked there because he found the body?"

"Yeah. Harry, I'm sorry I forgot to tell you."

"No problem. I'll speak with him as soon as I call this in and get a medical examiner out here, and notify the Criminal Investigation Division." Harry did just that before he stepped over to see Lennie. He couldn't bring himself to look toward the body as he passed.

"Not exactly what you'd want to find every morning, is it Lennie?"

"I should say not," replied Lennie in a low, scratchy voice. "What time did you find him, Lennie?"

"Oh, somewhere around 2:00 a.m., I guess. I'm not really sure."

"What were you doing out here then?"

"Well, if you really have to know, Harry, I was too drunk to drive out of here last night, so I pulled over near the boat launch and passed out. When I come to, I drove up over the top of the hill and found that." Lennie's shoulders hunched and he averted Harry's eyes as he swung his head toward Lester's body.

"What else did you see?"

"I didn't see nothin.'"

"Did you hear anything?" Harry's voice carried more authority and force, as if demanding a response.

"Christ, Harry, I think I told you, I passed out down by the landing, and when I came up, I saw that, and that's all I know."

"So…how did you get in touch with Ralph—do you have a cell phone?"

"No, I drove down to the Hatchery, pounded on their door, and used their phone. They had Ralph's number and so…" Lennie's voice trailed off.

Harry sighed deeply in frustration. He asked several more questions, and after getting no more from the older man, Harry said, "OK, Lennie, you can get out of here. I may need to talk to you later. See if you can stay sober for a while." Lennie mumbled something while he started his pickup, but the rumble from the cold motor made it impossible for Harry to understand what it was. Harry looked toward the body, shook his head, and closed his eyes as he realized that he would have to be the one to tell Betty Sawyer this dreadful news.

## CHAPTER 7

If it hadn't been for Jimmy White, Pat's evening would have ended in a total nightmare. They held each other tight; their nakedness kept them warm. Although Pat had never completely forgotten that Marge might burst through the door at any time, the intimacy she shared with this man whom she knew loved her was calming. They lay on top of the sheets, covered with a thin blanket, their lips pressed together tightly. His hands moved slowly over her firm breasts, and she responded by pulling herself against his hardness. Her breathing deepened while she slid her fingers through his thick hair, clenching her fists after filling them. They became entranced with the uncontrolled entwining of skin, hands, and lips, to embrace again in their deepest togetherness.

It was just past 3:00 a.m. Saturday morning when Marge stumbled into the cabin. Pat and Jimmy were wrapped tightly in each other's arms. Pat jumped at the first clicking sound of the doorknob, gently breaking the bond, moving toward the doorway, covering herself with a robe

"Where in hell have you been?" she asked as she poked her head into the kitchen.

"None of your goddamned business," replied Marge.

"I'm making it my business, and furthermore, that rifle you're carrying was in the corner where it's supposed to be when I left for the dance last night."

"Oh, you checked before leaving for the dance last night? I don't give a shit, little Pat bitch."

At the sound of the quarrel, Jimmy, startled out of sleep, curled himself into a defensive posture, prepared to defend himself. Confused by his strange surroundings, he'd forgotten where he was—in Pat's bed.

"What in the hell is going on?" Jimmy asked, sitting up, but still under the blanket. Marge had not noticed that Jimmy was tucked soundly under the covers of Pat's bed. When she did, she was startled into a verbal barrage against him. "What are you doin' here, you bastard? Get out of my house! Get out of my house! I'll kill you next, you bastard!"

—

At 5:30 a.m., the medical examiner's station wagon drove over the top of the knoll, followed by a state police vehicle. Harry recognized the driver immediately as Sgt. Tim Barnes, a trooper supervisor he had known for many years, but had not always enjoyed working with. Both Harry Circus and Tim Barnes were the same caliber of trooper, in that the law and their serious approach to justice superseded all else at times.

Harry walked toward the vehicles, and waited for them to come to a stop. The medical examiner was the first out, and immediately greeted Harry. "Good morning, Trooper Circus! What have we got?"

"We've got a goddamn mess, that's what." Harry turned quickly and walked toward Tim Barnes.

"So, how'd you end up way out here, Tim?"

In his cold, authoritative voice, the sergeant replied, "Not by choice."

"Well, look," Harry said, "the examiner should be here for a while. You're going to have a shitload of pictures to take. Do you mind sticking around until I get back?"

Barnes stuck his jaw out and frowned. "Where the hell are you going? This is your section of the woods, not mine."

"I know…it's just that I've… known Lester and his wife forever, and I just want to get down there and tell her as soon as I can.

"Well, I don't envy you that one. Sure, go ahead. I'll stay here till you get back." Harry walked slowly toward Ralph, who hadn't moved since Harry had arrived almost two hours earlier.

"Ralph, had you been home at all last night after the dance?" he asked.

"Oh yeah, Harry, I got home around midnight. It was a little warm at my place, so I thought I'd take a little ride past Davis Norton's to see if he made it home all right. Around 2:30 a.m., I got called by Lennie, and I met him out here."

"What was up with Davis?" Harry asked.

"Well, I'd never known Davis to be a drinkin' man, but he sure had a bunch of it last night. He and William Bradley got into it at the dance. I broke it up and went to get Davis a coffee, but when I got back, he was gone. I didn't see him again the rest of the night. He wasn't at his place when I went by."

"Look, I'm going down to tell Betty."

"Oh, God! I'm glad it's not me." He seemed to belch with the response.

"You get home, get some rest. I'll be by later. We'll have to compare notes. You'll be working closely with me on this one, Ralph."

"Okay, Harry, I'll see you later." Both men left in their own cars, Ralph following Harry over the gravel back to the tar. This time Harry was in no hurry to get to town. On his way, he thought of the many occasions such as church gatherings, or even the simple cashing of a check at the bank that would have allowed him to cross paths with Lester Sawyer. He wondered how he could find the right words to console Betty. Was there anything he could say to soften the blow? Oh, how he hated this part of his job. Telling an unsuspecting loved one of a tragedy, while being face to face with that pain. He wanted it to be done. The drive to town did not take very long.

Harry stopped the car at the beginning of Betty's driveway, and for a moment wondered if he'd be able to go through with this. He pushed the thought aside, and without further delay, he drove forward to the closed garage door and stopped the car. It looked as though Betty hadn't even gotten up yet, and as he rang the front door bell, the extreme quiet inside the house confirmed his thought. He rang the bell a second time, and heard footsteps from the room directly above the doorway at which he stood. A twitch of butterflies rose in his stomach. The staircase inside ended directly opposite the front door, and he heard footsteps descending the stairs.

With a slight fumbling of the doorknob, the door opened and Betty, in housecoat and slippers, stood before Harry Circus; a mix of concern and confusion on her face. "Harry! My goodness, what are you doing here so early in the morning?"

"Were you sleeping, Betty?" he asked softly.

"Yes, I was. Lester must be in the bathroom—otherwise he would have answered the door. Please come in, Harry." As he stepped through the door, he glanced at his watch. It was 6:30 a.m. She continued. "Is this about the alarm system that went off last night? You know, I didn't realize how tired I must have been, because I never heard Lester come back. He's such a dear lately. He never woke me up."

"Betty," Harry spoke at just above a whisper and was quickly interrupted.

"Lester," she called out. "Hurry down. Harry Circus is here. I swear he's worse than I am lately when he gets in that bathroom." Suddenly, as if being given her cue, she noticed the expression on the trooper's face. It was flushed. His eyes were sad. She now realized that he hadn't spoken more than just a few words since he'd arrived. "What is it, Harry? What's wrong?"

Harry called up his strength for the moment that evoked such dread. "Betty, Lester is not upstairs."

"What?"

"Betty....there's been..." He wanted to say "an accident," but that wasn't exactly true. "Lester is dead."

"You don't know what you're saying, Harry." At that moment, Harry noticed her knees buckling, and he lunged forward, grabbing only one arm, softening her fall to the floor. Betty was out cold.

Harry lifted her, intending to carry her to the couch in the living room. "Christ!" he remarked. "Either I'm going to have to start working out, or Betty needs to lose a little weight." He propped her head on a couple of pillows, then ran to the kitchen for a glass of cold water. As he returned, he could hear a faint moan. Betty seemed to be regaining consciousness. "Betty, drink some water." He lifted her head slightly so that she might swallow easily.

She took one large gulp, and in a gasping breath, lifted her head out of his hand and cried, "Lester, please, no. Lester, I need you, you can't be dead."

Harry remained calm and by her side as the reality of her loss sank in. He hoped she wouldn't faint again. "Betty, I want you to stay lying down here. I must make a phone call. I want someone to stay with you for a while." Harry went to the phone and dialed a number. The first ring was cut off as the call was answered—Annie must have been sitting with her hand on the receiver. "Hello?"

"Annie!"

"Harry. How are you doing?" The concern in her voice was calming.

"Oh, I'm all right, thanks. I wish I could say the same for Betty. It's awful, Annie. I just don't want to talk here, now. Betty is resting on the couch. I was wondering if you'd be able to come over and stay with her. She needs someone here."

"I'll be right over, Harry. I love you!"

"I love you, too, Annie. Please hurry." Harry heard the click of the receiver and put the handset back, then returned to Betty, who had not moved from her position. As he stood over her, he noticed the steady flowing line of a tear, trickling down the side of her face. He knew there were no words now that could alleviate her grief. He knew that a couple of hours with Annie would calm her somewhat, and he would return after speaking with the medical examiner at the scene.

It seemed inconceivable that Annie had driven the several miles between their homes in such a short time. Nevertheless, Harry was relieved to hear her soft voice as she entered through the front door after knocking ever so slightly. Her lips gently touched his cheek. "Hi, how's she doing?"

"She seems to be resting. I've not been able to speak a word to her since before you and I spoke on the phone."

"You're not thinking of questioning her right now, are you?"

"No, I was hoping you would stay with her while I head back up to the barrens. I'm sure there'll be a thousand unanswered questions out there." They spoke softly a few feet away from where Betty rested. Nothing they said was heard.

—

Across town, Ralph Bailey was lying on his bed in total exhaustion. The shock that had temporarily numbed his mind finally abated, allowing the vivid horror of what he had seen to pierce his very soul. His body jerked through spasms he could not control as he was thrust from a restless sleep to the wrenching hollow sounds of his empty, heaving stomach.

—

Harry had been gone less than two hours. When he returned to the boat landing and the scene of Lester's mutilation he found himself arriving at the very moment the local funeral director, who'd been called during Harry's absence, was placing the body onto a stretcher. By the time Harry had parked and gotten out of his car, the body of Lester Sawyer was in the body bag and zippered. The funeral director would transport the body to Augusta.

"What have you found out?" Harry asked the medical examiner.

"He died instantly from a single gunshot wound to the head. We'll get more from the autopsy in Augusta, but I think he was shot somewhere else and brought here for the rest of the dirty work. No signs of a struggle."

"That's the first thing I noticed when I pulled in this morning," responded Harry, "That and the fact that we couldn't find a trace of casings of any sort. It looks as though he was shot at close range. You said he died from a single bullet wound to the head?"

"Looks like it entered the left temple and exited just above the right, but like I said, Harry, let's wait 'till we get him to Augusta." Both men looked toward the marks left by a vehicle driving over what was known as a second year burn on the blueberry field. All that remained was the blackened earth, leaving no impressionable tire marks in the immediate area.

"Well, this looks like a good job for Ralph Bailey when he recovers." Harry said.

"I'm out of here, Harry. Keep in touch!"

"Yeah," was all that Harry said as he approached Tim Barnes, who was seated in his car. "Christ, did you even get out for a piss?" Harry asked dryly.

Barnes didn't respond. He looked at Harry with a somewhat bored, disgusted expression as he started his car and told Harry, "Oh, by the way, one of the sheriff's deputies found Lester Sawyer's car behind the bank. The rear of the bank is sealed off. The CID and the Major Crimes Unit will want to check the whole area." Harry simply nodded as the sergeant flipped a slight wave and left. Harry stood in the middle of the narrow dirt road watching the trooper drive away. He pursed his lips ironically, thinking, *"An attitude only a mother could love."*

He now knew that the inevitable time would arrive when he would have to face Betty again. He hoped he had made the right decision having Annie stay with her. Annie was good at things like this. *"If anyone could keep Betty calm by saying the right things, it was Annie",* he thought. He walked over the entire area one more time, looking for clues, and as far as he could see, all that remained was the blood-stained earth. The medical examiner had taken the wooden rack in his station wagon. That would be inspected by the Crime Lab in Augusta.

Harry walked toward his car, got in, and left the scene. Again, his thoughts were of Betty. The word of Lester's murder would spread quickly now by way of mouth through the little towns, where ears and tongues seemed to be much larger than the heads in which they'd been implanted. Upon the completion of Sgt. Barnes' report, the media would have their turn. Harry was so engrossed in his thoughts that several miles of gravel road went by unnoticed. Almost immediately after turning onto the pavement, the sky opened up and unleashed a downpour of rain, making it difficult to see more than several feet beyond the hood of his car. *"Good, I need more time to think,"* was Harry's silent response to the rain.

He felt very distracted, as if ten thoughts were running through his mind all at once. He recalled his conversation with old Walter up on Rt. 193: *"Looks like 30/30 to me, Harry!"* And his question to William Bradley at the corner variety: *"Have you been selling much 30/30 ammo lately?"* Christ, what was all this talk about shooting all of a sudden? His gut only offered him more questions. He wondered what Betty had meant when she'd asked if his being there was about the alarm system that went off last night. *"What alarm system? What could she have meant by that?"*

He quickly jotted down notes while he drove. His speed never exceeded 45 mph. He looked straight ahead through the pelting rain as his thoughts went back to last night when he and Annie had been wound tightly together through body and soul, alone and quiet. The hours seemed to pass like minutes. Such a short time together, until the deafening ring of the phone that woke them and offered such dreadful news.

Harry had not yet arrived in town when word of Lester's gruesome demise began spreading quickly through absurd rumors that ranged from satanic sacrifice to cannibalism—just the type of thing that Harry feared would happen, yet something he had no control over. The same thought had entered Annie's mind shortly after Harry had left this morning. She'd taken the precaution of removing the receiver of Betty's phone from its cradle to prevent any fool who'd heard of Lester's death from trying to contact Betty, and wasting the poor woman completely before Harry could return to question her further and possibly shed more light on what had actually happened. Annie now sat next to Betty holding one of her hands gently in hers. Betty had regained her composure. Just as Annie thought the timing might be right for questions, she heard the thump of a car door, and hoped it was Harry.

—

Harry's questioning of Betty Sawyer went on for hours, Annie stayed close at the request of not only her husband, but the newly widowed wife of the deceased and their good friend. Nothing that Betty offered, however, made any sense of her claim about the early morning call that sent Lester to the bank to silence an unreported alarm. Finally, Harry, at the signaling of his wife, realized that it was time to leave the poor woman to her thoughts of grief and the consideration of upcoming funeral arrangements.

## CHAPTER 8

THE GRAY, DISTANT SUN SHINING dull through an overcast sky greeted a multitude of mourners filing through the black wrought-iron gate of the small town cemetery. Many familiar faces bore the stress and sorrow always experienced with the loss of a close friend, the feelings seemingly contagious as they spread from face to face. The hems of black dresses swayed slightly in the light breeze. The gray granite stones clashed with the green late summer grasses, while the spotted bunches of flowers adorned the monuments, remembering loved ones of yesteryear. Somehow, the color black was fitting for this quiet grieving place. The mourners encircled the final resting place; the faint sobbing of the most recent widow held everyone captive, while all hoped for an enlightening eulogy.

For the first time in many a year, Harry Circus wore a fitted three-piece gray suit, black tie, and black highly polished wing-tips that gave him more the look of a young banker than of a seasoned state police trooper. From his position, slightly elevated and facing the congregated mourners, he searched the faces before him. His mind would not allow him to dismiss the possibility that one of the mourners might very well be a murderer. It was unfortunate, he thought, that Betty was unable to offer anything that might have shed light on the events of that dreadful Friday evening when he questioned her Saturday morning on his return from the murder scene. Unless Lester was involved with something or someone from out of town, the murderer was probably a local, and most likely someone that both Lester and Harry knew very well.

Annie noticed that her husband's mind was a thousand miles away, and she tugged him back to reality with a gentle pull of his arm. Disdainfully, he returned to a rigid posture and focused on the tall, thin minister who began by asking the mourners to join him in prayer. Harry could not help himself from being distracted from the slow, progressing eulogy. His naturally suspicious nature would not allow him to dismiss the feeling that someone here, within his very reach was, a murderer. His eyes scanned each face—faces he'd seen and would see as long as he represented the law in this and the surrounding communities.

He vowed that he would leave no stone unturned. He would never allow himself to shy away from questioning anyone he felt the need to question. He made this promise as he looked upon the silver casket that held the body of his long-time friend, Lester Sawyer.

—

It was mid-morning. Pat seemed unable to move from her seat near the window. Her mind, locked to the thought of the funeral now taking place, a funeral for a man whom she'd only felt abhorrence; in her opinion, a true demagogue, suddenly forced her to remember the many times that she'd been snubbed or completely ignored by Lester whenever she was in the company of poor old Marge. *"Marge!"* Fear rose from the pit of her stomach. *"Oh, God! Where had she gone off to Friday evening? What had she done with that goddamned 30/30 of hers?"* Vividly now, the vision on Friday night of Marge's threats toward Jimmy came back to her. She saw again in her mind's eye Marge's rifle leveled at Lennie's head. *"Was Marge capable of killing a person?"* She knew she must now guard her own safety first. She had to regain Marge's confidence again, believing strongly that Marge would eventually share with her where she'd been on Friday night.

As Pat raised her cup to her lips and realized her coffee had gone cold, she grimaced as she placed the cup down and saw something out of the corner of her eye. With a slight jerk of her head, she quickly looked out the window in the direction of that movement. It was Marge, coming toward the cabin along the edge of the driveway. She held her favorite 30/30 rifle grasped in her fist, her arm extended fully to her side. Her corncob pipe was clinched between her teeth. Again, a flutter of nerves erupted from the pit of Pat's stomach.

"Oh shit, all I wanted was a little more time." Before the words themselves could be absorbed by the quiet of the cabin, the door was flung open, and in came Marge with a heavy pounding of her boots as she tried to dislodge an accumulation of dry mud caked on from her morning walk along the riverbank.

"Good mornin', little Pat. How we doin' this mornin'?"

"Fine, Marge, how are you doing?"

"Oh, I'm just fine too, little Pat. Want some coffee?"

"No, I'm fine, thanks. Where were you off to so early this morning?" As soon as the words came out, Pat's eyes rolled backwards in anticipation of the expected barrage that would follow.

"Well, don't we just have to know everything about Marge lately, little Pat? I don't see you getting up early and coming with me, and when I come back, I don't ask you questions about what you do and where you go! Well, do I? Do I?"

"I didn't mean anything by it, Marge. I was only making conversation, that's all." Pat took a deep breath. "Marge, how long have we been friends?"

"Well, we've been friends ever since Harvey died. We've been together that long anyway."

"Right!" responded Pat. In the back of her mind however, she held the secret. "When have I ever done anything to harm you? Haven't I always been on your side?" Marge simply stood staring into Pat's eyes, saying nothing. From the look on Marge's face, Pat knew that just the right coaxing might open her up enough for Pat to get the answers she needed to satisfy her curiosity.

—

As the eulogist progressed sluggishly, Davis Norton, who had not been seen since his fight Friday night, was lying with his face buried deep into his pillow. He was still very ill from a three-day battle with Jack Daniels, unable to face daylight and the pain it would produce. Reality, it seemed, was just a dream in his not yet fully awakened mind. He moaned and moved ever so slightly, while the throbbing within his head made him nauseous, and he wanted to vomit. The sickness, however, was not solely the result from the abuse of alcohol. The truth and the horror of his actions in the early morning hours on Saturday made him far more ill than any hangover could ever cause, but the secret he held deep within his consciousness, he shared with someone he knew. It was the core of his sickness. As of yet however, neither of them knew their secret would soon be shared.

The knock on the downstairs door felt like a direct pound from hell. Knocking, knocking, it wouldn't stop. Slowly Davis went toward his closed bedroom door, reaching out, his vision still blurred through heavily moistened, hung-over eyes and grasped the doorknob, opening the door. The knocking continued on his way down the stairs as Davis's quivering voice called out, "Hold on to your hat, I'm coming!" He swung the door open, and before him stood Ralph Bailey, shit eatin' grin and all.

"Morning, Davis," was all he was able to get out. To his total surprise, Davis slammed the door in his face.

"What the hell is eatin' you, Davis?" Ralph yelled through the door as he heard Davis's retreating footsteps stumbling on the stairs. "Davis, I want you to open this door right now! Do you hear me? Open this door!" Ralph strained to hear any movement from inside. *"What in hell crawled up his butt?"* Ralph thought to himself. He began knocking again on the door, but now the knocking took on a more authoritative and demanding sound that shattered the quiet of the country yard. Ralph took several steps backwards off the step, and looked upward toward the windows of the second story. The shades were drawn tightly against the sills, blocking his view. He tried to think back to Friday night during and after the fight between Davis and William, and wondered if there was something that he might have done to turn Davis's anger toward him. The more he thought about it, the more he came up with nothing. Nothing he did should have turned Davis against him.

From somewhere in the upstairs part of the house, Ralph could hear the sounds of something being dragged across the floor and then dropped, dragged then dropped. It was impossible to know exactly what it was that Davis was doing in there, but it sounded rather strange from his position in front of the house. He decided to check the rear of the building, but there was no rear exit. As Ralph returned to the front, he heard the destructive sound of smashing glass and a heavy dead weight thumping on the ground. He began running along the side of the house, for twenty or thirty feet, and slowed his pace while cautiously approaching the front corner. His hand firmly grasped the grip of his pistol, in case it needed to be pulled, and he peered around the corner, seeking the cause of the crash.

—

Irene was standing no more than ten feet from Lester's widow, and appeared sedated. She wore a dark brown pantsuit with a tiny violet pinned to the lapel. Her eyes were concealed with a pair of very dark, large-rimmed sunglasses that seemed fitting, yet somewhat out of place on such a dull, dreary day. The farthest thing from her mind was whether anyone took notice.

Someone had taken notice. It was Darcy, the hot-coffee-slinging teller who really didn't like either Lester or Irene. Standing across from the widow, Darcy's cold stare could have pierced steel. She knew what had gone on at the bank, day after day. Irene had been Lester's pet thing. Darcy hated them both. It was over now. No more fooling around for Lester the snake. Darcy's eyes became two thin lines as she squinted, trying to see through Irene's dark glasses. As if touched by Darcy's eyes, Irene felt suddenly uneasy, as if someone was watching her, knowing her very thoughts. Irene breathed an uneven, quivering breath, moving her eyes under the concealment of the lenses. *"Guilt, that's all. No one knew about Lester and me,"* she thought. *"They only suspected. No one actually knew."*

Then their eyes met—Irene's puffy, concealed eyes and Darcy's cold, squinting ones. Irene felt them going directly through her. "That little trouble-maker," Irene whispered inaudibly to the ears that surrounded her. "Why is she staring at me? I've never done anything to her. What the hell's her problem?"

As her voice began to rise, the elderly woman to her left, whom she did not recognize, asked "What dear?"

Sarcastically, Irene responded, "Mind your own business, I'm praying." The old woman merely stared, taken completely off guard. From his position, Harry Circus was able to hear Irene's harsh remark to the elderly woman. It seemed to him rather out of place that she should be anything but passive, as he had been made aware of the affair between Lester and Irene. Because of his position as the locally based trooper, whether he wanted to be or not, he became the ears for every little tidbit of gossip that titillated the local rumormongers. He was now mentally making his list of those to be questioned. *I will leave no stone unturned. I will shy away from no question, if I feel it should be asked. No one will be overlooked.*

He thought about Betty, how he would do his best to keep her from knowing of the affair, but if it came down to it, all that mattered to Harry was personally escorting the assassin to their cell.

The tall, thin minister bid his final farewell to Lester Sawyer. "Rest in peace, my friend," he said, while a single sobbing infiltrated an absolute hush that had fallen over the mourners.

Slowly the mourners began to exit through the same wrought-iron gate while the minister clung to the hand of Betty Sawyer. Annie tried to move in the direction of the widow, but her movement was suddenly stopped by Harry's tugging on her arm. "I was only going to pay my respects, Harry."

"No problem, Annie. I was simply going to ask you to meet me at the car."

"Oh, all right. Are you sure you won't come with me?"

"I'll be seeing Betty first thing in the morning, so it can wait. There are other people I need to see as soon as possible." Then he turned and immediately walked away. Annie merely shook her head slightly, knowing how Harry's attitude would change now as he became totally subjective toward his investigation surrounding the murder. Nothing Annie could say or do could dissuade Harry from his goal. She could see it in his face, feel it in his grasp. She would wait for him and offer him her full support.

As Harry came to within sight of his vehicle, he noticed William Bradley, his right arm gesturing for him to hurry. With the other hand, thumb straight up, baby finger extended toward the mouth as to indicate Harry's car radio had been signaling. A fever began to throb suddenly through Harry's veins as he started running toward his car. Thanking William, he excused himself as he slid behind the wheel, shutting the door behind him, causing a scowl to form on the young man's face.

"This is Harry." From the speaker he heard Ralph Bailey's voice.

"Harry, we have a problem."

"Where are you, Ralph?"

In a very, stressed, anxious tone, Ralph's voice returned to the speaker. "Harry, I'm in front of Davis Norton's. That fool's barricaded himself in there and he's been shooting at me. He blew the goddamn windshield out of my car."

"Stay low, don't do anything, Ralph. I'll be right there."

—

After several seconds, Marge remained gazing into Pat's eyes. Pat, still very uncomfortable, realized that as calm as Marge now was, there would be no better time to begin some light, easy questions. "Maybe I will have another cup with you, Marge."

"Sure enough, little Pat, plenty left and still hot." Slowly they drank their coffee, exchanging thoughts about the weather, eels, and hunting. Pat's desire to recapture Marge's confidence overflowed with enthusiasm. Pat wanted this opportunity to assure herself that Marge was not capable of killing anyone. It had to be now.

"Marge, did you know that Lester Sawyer was found up on the barrens Saturday morning, dead?"

"What! That old fart dead? What happened to him, shit his pants and die from the stink?" She immediately began laughing.

Pat shook her head and closed her eyes, emitting a faint smile. "No, Marge, he was murdered. Shot in the head, from what I've heard." Marge's laughter ended as swiftly as it had begun, and her face turned serious.

—

Annie turned quickly, hearing the tires squeal, and all that she saw was the blue blur of Harry's car as it sped away through the thick growth of trees at the cemetery's entrance. "What the......" she muttered at the sight.

Harry was doing eighty in less than a quarter mile from the cemetery gate; the blue strobe lights penetrated the dullness of the day. One-handed, he maneuvered the car through the curves and straight stretches of the narrow backcountry roads. The other hand and thumb were pressed firmly on the radio's mike button. "It's Harry. I've just been advised by Constable Bailey of a 1032", (police code for shots have been fired). He's at Davis Norton's. At that point he gave the location of the shooting.

"What's Ralph doing?" a voice crackled from the speaker.

"I've told him to stay down and do nothing until I get there," Harry responded.

"Where are you now, Harry?"

"I'm about five minutes ETA from Ralph."

"Okay, Harry, I'm on my way." The voice belonged to Sgt. Tim Barnes.

—

A small patch of clouds had broken up, allowing a solid beam of rays to shine directly on the red and blue lights of Ralph Bailey's police car, intensifying the colors and giving the impression they were lit. Ralph lay on the ground beside the opened driver's door to maintain radio contact with the troopers who were now, as far as Ralph felt, way overdue. No way did he want the responsibility for this one; besides, from the sounds of Davis's barrage at the glass of his cruiser, his little .380 backup pistol would do him no justice. As the words "Where in hell are you, Harry?" barely passed his lips, he turned at the sound of squealing tires as the blue car and its penetrating blue strobes rounded the final curve about a hundred yards from Davis Norton's. At almost the same instant that he heard Harry's car, from the opposite direction he saw the nearly inverted reflection of Tim Barnes' vehicle appear as a mirage in the distance.

Harry brought his vehicle to a stop next to Ralph's, leaving enough room for him to open his door, creating another barricade between the two police vehicles. He slid low out of the seat and joined Ralph on the ground facing the house. Ralph seemed surprised that no gunshots were fired toward Harry as he pulled alongside, but his stare seemed focused on Harry's suit.

"How long has it been since he's fired at you?" Harry hollered.

"Well, the last shot from the house took my windshield out, and that was very shortly before I talked to you on the radio. There were no shots after that." Just then, Barnes' vehicle veered suddenly at the rear of Harry's car, blocking off the remainder of the road. Tim Barnes slid in between both officers, asking for an update on the situation. Harry told Ralph to explain the events as they had developed, but as the constable began, another intense barrage of gunfire from the house pelted all three police vehicles.

"Fucking...buckshot!" The words wheezed from Tim Barnes' mouth. "Has anyone tried talking to him yet?" he asked.

"I got here a few seconds before you did," Harry said. At that point, Barnes cupped his hands around his mouth to assume the shape of a megaphone, asking Davis if he could hear him. From inside the house, a subdued, muffled voice could be heard, yet it was not clear what was being said.

"I can't hear what you're say..." Before the sergeant could finish, several more shots were fired in their direction, forcing all three to duck again, low between the vehicles. "If I can't get him to talk, the shit's gonna hit the fan soon. Does anyone know what might have brought this on? I thought Davis was a quiet old fart. Never had any problems with him, have we?" Barnes asked.

Harry spoke up. "As long as I've known him, I guess the biggest thing with him was heading out to camp, that's about it."

Ralph spoke up. "Well, like I told you, Harry, last Friday night at the dance, he was really loaded and got into that fight with William Bradley. That's the first time I've ever had a problem with him, that's why I came over today. I wanted to see if he was all right." Ralph relayed the events that had led up to the first shots earlier this morning.

"You don't..." Harry stopped.

"What?" responded the sergeant.

"Really, it was nothing," Harry said.

"Don't keep any pieces out now, Harry—any piece to this puzzle might fit, you know that."

"Well, it all seems to be happening a little too fast here. Let's go back a little. Friday night, Davis shows up at the dance drunk, and gets into a fight. Saturday morning we find Lester Sawyer dead and gutted, now this. I mean, come on, what if they're tied in somehow?"

"I don't see any direct connection, Harry, but until we get old

89

Davis up there to calm down and do a little chatting, it's not going to do us any good to assume anything. Is there anyone that you know that's close to him that may be able to talk him down from there?"

"As far as I know, Tim, he's all alone." Ralph said.

Still unaware of the events taking place, and the danger in which her husband was in, Annie Circus graciously accepted Betty Sawyer's invitation to return with her to her home for some light refreshments. Betty seemed rather composed now, possibly the effects of a sedative she'd taken to get her through the tough part, the funeral. *"Their marriage is over,"* Annie thought. *"All those years you spend with someone, all the ups and downs, the good and the bad. In a split second, a life is over. All that's left are memories and a few pictures."* Annie's mind raced. *"Where could Harry be? I hope he's safe. Why couldn't he have at least told me he was leaving, said good-bye or something?"* Her eyes drifted toward the silver casket surrounded by large bunches of flowers. *"Why couldn't he have just said good-bye?"*

—

Tim Barnes looked toward the two men. "I'm going to try to talk to him again. We must do everything we can to end this without bloodshed." Both men nodded in agreement. Tim cupped his hands again in the direction of the house. "Davis! This is Tim Barnes. Talk to me, Davis! You don't want to hurt anyone and no one wants to hurt you. Come on Davis, talk to me." The veins bulged in his neck under the force he expended, as there was a distance of about thirty feet from the front of the building and the area between the vehicles where the three men lay protected.

All three men heard Davis's strained voice respond to the sergeant from within the house. "I don't want to hurt anyone. I

90

didn't kill 'im, he was already dead!"

"Did you hear that?" Ralph asked.

"I sure did," replied Barnes. "Davis, come on out and let's talk about it. No one will hurt you. You have my word on that. Come downstairs and open the door. Just leave your guns up there, okay?" The silence became sickening. The wait seemed an eternity. After an hour, movement was seen by all three through the only lifted window shade in the house.

Suddenly, the front door opened slowly, and a very tired, filthy looking Davis Norton appeared. Clenched tightly in his right hand was a book. The other hand was empty. His stained white T-shirt was tucked into the left side of his green work trousers, yet it hung to below the pocket of his right side, and he was wearing moccasins. He stood on the top step, just outside of the door.

"Relax Davis," Tim Barnes sounded out. "Everything's going to be all right, stay right where you are." Tim Barnes was the only officer to carry his pistol. The other two men's eyes were a frantic movement in Davis's direction that would have alerted them to any danger. As the three officers came to within several feet of the front door, Tim gestured to his officers to stop and he spoke gently to Davis. "Davis, I want you to step down onto the grass, and give the book to Harry. Can you do that for me?"

Without speaking, Davis took the two steps down, and handed the book to Harry, saying, "It's all in there, Harry." Harry passed the book to Ralph and then took several steps so that he stood inches away from Davis's face. He grasped Davis's left wrist, pulling it slightly toward him, and turned him around, immediately informing him of his right to remain silent. As Harry continued explaining and placing the cuffs, belonging to Barnes on his wrists, Tim Barnes motioned to Ralph to follow him inside. What they found stopped them dead in their tracks. Davis Norton had stockpiled an arsenal of weapons and ammunition. It would be difficult at a glance to determine an actual count. The room he had barricaded himself in was filled with high-powered rifles, shotguns, and pistols of every caliber imaginable, and a cache of ammo for each. Had it been his intention to hole up and fight, Davis Norton could have conceivably held the authorities off for days.

Minutes after the first shots had been fired, word spread rapidly through the small towns. Several rumors had the gunman dead, another had all three officers wounded and in serious condition. Annie heard the first of the rumors while she was with Betty Sawyer and her family. Refusing to be coaxed into hysteria, though visibly anxious, she walked calmly to the telephone, placing a call to the troop headquarters. She identified herself and requested an update on the situation. Annie smiled with relief as the concerned voice on the telephone assured her that no one had been hurt, and a suspect had been taken into custody. She remained standing by the telephone after hanging up relieved at the news. Suddenly, it began to ring. It was Harry.

"Harry, you're all right!" Annie whispered into the mouthpiece.

Harry responded with, "no problem babe!"

"It's so good to hear your voice."

"Yeah, it's good to hear yours, too, Annie."

"There were a lot of rumors going around, so I called headquarters and...."

Harry interrupted, "No problem, I'll be home as soon as I can. Annie, this may take a while."

"I love you, Harry!"

"Yeah... me too, Annie. See you as soon as I can." Annie heard the receiver click and he was gone.

"Good-bye Harry," she whispered, and hung up. She turned, smiling to everyone in the room. "Harry's all right, they're all okay."

—

The questioning of Davis Norton began immediately upon Harry's return from the telephone. Davis had previously waived his right to an attorney while being questioned at the scene of the shooting. When they got to the Washington County Jail in Machias, he was a man out of his senses. He babbled on that it was all in the book. "It's all in the book, Harry...it's all in the book!" Although, each time Harry asked where in the book, he received the same response: "I didn't kill 'im; he was already dead. It's in the book Harry, all in the book." The routine went on for several hours. Harry's patience was non-yielding.

Then, unexpectedly, Davis began to cry, whimpering like a child scolded into defeat by a relentless parent. Harry sat opposite Davis at the large table and watched as a man whom he'd known for many years fell apart before him. It was best, Harry thought, to leave him for a time. He was hoping that the crying would loosen up Davis's ability to talk about the events over the past several days.

Harry stepped through the door of the interrogation room into a dimly lit hall. The leather heels of his wing-tips clacked against the floor tiles. The bare plaster walls painted with high gloss enamel and the hanging white globe light fixtures accentuated the building's antiquity. Barnes looked up from his paperwork at the sound of the approaching footsteps.

"How's it going in there, Harry?"

"He just broke down, crying like a baby," Harry said.

"Is that a good sign?"

"Yeah, that's why I left him for a while; I'll give him a few minutes, then go back in with some coffee and a fresh pack of cigarettes. I think he might be ready to talk then."

"Good," answered Barnes. "Anything about that book?"

"Not yet, but like I said, give him a little more time and maybe, then." The echoes of distant voices from another part of the building could be heard now, and both men's inquisitive natures were revealed as they looked in that general direction.

"Look, Harry, you want me to go in there and give it a shot? You've been at it since we brought him in here this morning."

Harry flicked his left arm upward slightly and out, sliding his shirtsleeve up, exposing his watch. "7:00 p.m. Christ, I never realized it was that late. I probably ought to send for sandwiches with those coffees and butts." Harry spoke at just above a whisper.

"Look, Harry, I'm almost done here. I'll run down to the corner. What kind of smokes do you want?" Barnes asked.

"I think he smokes Camels, you know, the small non-filtered kind, couple of burgers, two regular coffees. I need the sugar." Both men laughed in agreement, as Harry stretched in an attempt to relieve some of his fatigue and frustration. Harry looked in the direction of the tiny room that held Davis Norton, and couldn't help but wonder if all of these events tied into each other. Over and over again, they came to him in his mind. *"Friday night's dance and fight. Lester's midnight phone call and eventual murder. The shootout this morning. Davis's consistent babbling about the book and not being the one who had killed Lester."* They all tied in somehow. He was convinced of that, and the old man sitting behind that varnished oak door would shortly begin placing crucial parts of this bizarre puzzle into place. He hoped.

—

Irene entered through her front door still dazed and out of touch with reality. It was over for her, she felt. How could she go back to the bank? How could she look into or simply walk through Lester's office, remembering the times they'd shared? She knew most people wouldn't understand how they felt toward each other and their need to be together. Before even taking her coat off, she stood before the large maple hutch, and watched the scotch cascade slowly over the ice until the glass was full. She drank deeply, closing her eyes, allowing the warmth to caress her; knowing that shortly the pain would be dulled. She quickly filled the glass once more, and walked toward the love seat that faced a large bow window overlooking her gardens—the seat she'd shared with her lover on the nights he was able to spend with her when they would have both otherwise been alone.

"He loved me," she whispered softly. The effects of the scotch took hold, closing her eyes; her head tilted slightly back, she breathed and felt her lungs fill with the essence from the whiskey. "I feel so alone!" she cried. "How can I go on without him? It can never be the same for me. Why should I continue living when the only man I ever, truly loved is dead?" Dead. The reality of the word burned her soul.

Irene's body jerked at the first sound of the telephone's chime. The last thing she wanted was to talk on the phone. It kept ringing. She shook her head as if it hurt her ears, then turned quickly, and as she did, the glass slipped from her hand, smashing on the hardwood floor. She gasped, screaming at the phone to stop ringing. Reaching out, she tore the receiver from its cradle, wanting to fling it across the room to have it smash against the red bricks of the fireplace. Instead, she brought it to her ear and said, "Hello."

Without speaking a single word, the caller broke the connection, bringing the loathsome silence of an open line into Irene's ear.

—

Davis devoured the sandwich in several large bites, swallowing each with large gulps of hot coffee. Harry watched in amazement, and would have offered his burger, but felt rather ill since it had been twelve hours since he himself had eaten. Neither man spoke during their supper. Immediately upon completion of his, Davis reached for the pack of Camels, opened it, and lit one. After breathing the smoke in deeply, as if he'd sucked it down to his toes, he exhaled as he looked toward Harry and said, "Thanks."

Harry nodded his head in response. "Doing a little better, Davis?"

"Yeah, I haven't been able to get anything down for a couple of days."

Harry's voice now took on coarseness, directness with the first question. "Can you help me out here, Davis? You've been saying a lot of things that don't add up, like, I didn't kill him, he was already dead, and it's all in the book." What does this mean? Davis, come on, work with me here."

Davis again drew deeply from what now was a half-burned cigarette. He exhaled a deep sigh filled with smoke, and began. "I went out to camp last Friday morning. I had intended to stay all weekend. I had a few bottles of Jack." He coughed a half laugh. "You know, I'd hang out, and do a little fishin', some target shootin'." Harry nodded his head to indicate he understood. Davis began again. "I got out there, Harry, and them miserable bastards had clear-cut every goddamned tree, as far as I could see." Davis's voice rose with each syllable. "There wasn't a goddamned thing left, Harry."

"Take it easy, we'll cover everything, Davis."

"Yeah, I know, I just freak out every time I think of it. That was the family camp, Harry. We had a lot of good times there. How could they have been so cold and not left a single goddamned tree?" Harry felt his frustration.

"Go on, Davis, you're doing fine." Harry looked at his watch: 7:54 p.m. He took a breath and exhaled slowly, thinking how long the night was going to be.

Davis lit another smoke and took several deep drags before speaking again. "Well, I sat around there a while—I think I just lost it, I'm not sure. I even forgot where I was for a time. I remember the sun was hot on my face while I sat there, but it didn't feel good. Then I started drinking, and the more I drank, the angrier I got. Then I left."

"About what time did you leave?"

"Oh, I'm not really sure, maybe around four, five in the afternoon. Yeah, that's what it was… five!"

"Are you sure?" Harry asked.

"Yeah, I'm sure."

"Then what did you do?"

"Well, I kept drinking, finished the first bottle on my way out from that shit hole and headed back to town."

"Did you come right back?"

"Yeah, I drove back to the house, got drunk."

Harry snickered, "You mean you weren't drunk yet?"

Davis stared slyly at Harry, but said nothing.

"How long did you stay at the house?"

"I'm not sure what time it was when I left. It was well after dark."

"Where'd you go?"

"I drove around for a while, nowhere special. Then I ended up at the VF…I got pounded or something."

Harry spoke. "Think about it, Davis. What happened at the dance?" Davis reached for the pack of cigarettes, and for the first time since he'd been with Harry in the room, he noticed the book. "Where'd you get that book, Harry?"

"Don't you remember? You gave it to me this morning, and you kept repeating, 'It's all in the book. Harry, it's all in the book.'"

Davis breathed deeply. "Yeah, I remember now. You want to

know what it was I was talking about."

"I'd love to." Harry breathed a sigh of relief. Davis flipped through the pages to a short story he'd read many years ago. "I can't make out who wrote it", he said and turned the opened book toward Harry.

"*Trilogy of a Forest.*" "It was everything they did out there to the camp. It was all down in words. When I saw the place, the story came back to me, and I snapped."

Harry looked at it for a moment, then said, "Can I keep it for a while and read it later? I'll give it back to you as soon as I'm done."

"Yeah, no problem. You'll see, Harry." Then Davis merely looked down, shaking his head, wiping away a single tear that ran down his cheek.

"Go on," Harry said, "you're doing fine. Now what about the dance? Do you remember getting to the dance?"

"Yeah, I remember getting there and starting to walk across the dance floor mindin' my own business, and that little fuckhead, William, knocked me on my ass. Before I could get back up, he knocked me on my ass again. I remember someone helping me up onto a chair, then I left. That's all I remember."

"That's all you remember of the dance, you mean?" Harry asked.

"Yeah."

"Then what happened?"

"It's pretty foggy after that. I didn't get far. I drove as far as the bank, pulled in behind the building, and passed out."

"How long were you out?" Harry asked quickly.

"I haven't got a clue, but when I came to, oh God..." Davis began gagging as if he would vomit. "I didn't kill him! He was already dead when I found him."

"Relax, Davis, you're doing very well, just relax." Harry continued calmly. "Tell me what you did when you came to." A long minute of silence passed.

"Well, I got out and pissed, and when I came back to the truck, I thought I saw something over by the teller's window. I went over to take a look. And there's Sawyer, with a fuckin' hole in his head."

"Was he dead when you found him?"

"Goddamned right he was dead. Had a fuckin' hole, right through his head, I told you."

"Yeah, I know what you told me, but did you make any attempt to check, you know, a pulse, or anything?"

"Harry, for Christ's sake.... Look, I'm not going to lie to ya, I hated that sleazy, shit bastard for everything he did to me and Irene."

"Irene?" Harry asked. "Irene from the bank?" A long held secret was about to be told.

"Yeah, most people didn't know, but we were going to get married before she got that job working for that little shit bastard, then when he came into the picture, that was it for us. I hated that bastard."

"Okay, go back a little. You found the body near the drive-up, then what?"

"I laughed, okay, I laughed, but I wanted more. I picked him up, dragged him to the truck and lifted him into the back. I wasn't sure what I'd do with him yet, but on my way out to the barrens and after a couple more pulls on the Jack, I knew."

"So you tied him to the rack and gutted him?" Harry's voice rose louder with each word, as a wave of nausea hit him.

"Yeah, I gutted the little pig!"

*CHAPTER 9*

---

THE LONG, SLEEPLESS NIGHT WAS ENDING. Harry's eyes felt as large as two silver dollars that had been left on his pillow overnight. The early morning light filtering through the drawn blinds made him stir restlessly, but as he moved to glance at the clock, he was careful not to disturb Annie, who he thought was still fast asleep.

"What time is it?" she asked softly.

In a voice bordering on a whisper, Harry merely replied, "Five-thirty." They had very little time when Harry returned home last evening. He did however, tell her, but not all of what took place at the jail and Davis' confession.

Knowing that Harry needed to get up, Annie turned slowly and said, "I'll make coffee." Harry never turned, he only smiled. His mind was on one thing. He reached for the phone and dialed Ralph's number. As the sound of the ring came to his ear, Harry's thoughts went back to last night and Davis's confession. It was difficult to accept that Davis had been capable of committing such a hideous act to another human being; regardless of the fact the other person had already been dead.

At that moment, he heard the sound of the receiver being lifted up, and Ralph's sleepy voice on the other end. "Hello, Ralph here."

"Rise and shine Constable. I need you to come out to the barrens early this morning. We need to cover that site again—there has to be something we've missed."

"Well, I can be at your place by six-o'clock."

"Great, come on over, have some coffee, and we'll leave from here." Without saying good-bye, Harry hung the receiver back into its cradle and got dressed.

A few minutes later, Harry was impatiently downing what was left of his first cup of coffee while shaving when he heard the sound of Ralph's car coming up the drive. Looking at his watch, he was pleased with Ralph's punctuality. Ralph knocked once, and walked in. He greeted Annie, who was seated at the table directly across from him. Her hands were wrapped around the huge coffee mug, warming them against the early morning chill that always seemed to engulf the kitchen area.

"Good morning, Ralph. Help yourself to a cup, it's hot." As he approached the pot, the smell of freshly brewed coffee made his stomach growl because he had neglected to eat, not wanting to be late. He could hear Harry's electric shaver in the next room, and relaxed somewhat thinking he may even get a chance to enjoy one cup.

As the shaver clicked off, Harry called, "Let me fill you in on what went on last night, Ralph." He came into the kitchen, and began relaying the statements Davis had made, and his eventual confession. "That brings us to two crime scenes, Constable."

"So," Ralph responded, "Davis said he found Lester at the bank, dead. Lennie found him on the barrens. You think Lennie's involved?"

"Hell, no! His statement fits. He was drunk and passed out up there, that's the end of that. I'm not real sure I believe Davis completely. We have to stop at the bank and give it the once over. The drive-up window won't open 'til eight-thirty. The CID released the area. That gives us two hopefully uninterrupted hours. Let's make the best of it." Harry strapped his holster around his waist, giving Annie the same shivering up the spine she got every time that gun hung from his hip. Harry walked to the coffee pot and filled his mug again. He motioned for Ralph to do the same, and Ralph jumped up to comply. Annie looked up, and was kissed coldly on the forehead. "Are you staying home all day?" Harry asked.

"I will if you need me here for anything. If not, I thought I would spend some time with Betty."

"No…that's fine, Annie. I think it's great. She needs all the support we can give her. If I need you, I'll call here first." As he turned to walk away, Annie rose and tugged at his arm, took one step, and pulled him into an embrace. "Be careful today, Harry. I love you."

Not wanting to be romantic in front of the constable, Harry responded with, "I'm always careful, baby, you know that." Then, he lightly squeezed Annie's shoulder as he turned and walked out of the door.

—

Davis Norton's confession gave the police the lead they needed to steer the investigation in a new direction. Knives and firearms were removed from Davis's home, and sent to the crime lab for testing. The results would confirm his statement, leading investigators toward a murder suspect if in fact there was another person involved. While these and other events of the investigation were taking place, Davis lay on his bunk in a cell, staring at the paint-chipped ceiling, feeling no regret for what he had done. His mind raced back to that Friday when he had found the camp, and that alone was his only regret. The fact that Lester Sawyer was dead, and his body desecrated by his own hand was of no concern to him.

—

The bank was a short drive from Harry's. Ralph was daydreaming, and with a sudden jerk, he felt the vehicle stop. Harry began barking out instructions. "Constable, I want you to start over in that far corner," pointing in the direction that Davis indicated he'd been parked when he first noticed the body.

"What am I looking for, Harry?"

"Anything—an empty beer bottle, a whiskey bottle, a snot rag. Here, take this plastic bag and gloves. You find something, put it in, zip-lock it." With bag in hand, Ralph walked slowly toward the far corner, his eyes scanning every cubic inch of black-top. Moving slowly, Harry scanned the area where Davis told him he'd found Lester. As he walked, his mind formed the picture of Lester stretched out on the rack. Slowly he passed the area where the residual powder of bloody, shattered glass had been found, sending a cold sensation through his veins.

He was approaching the edge of the lot some twenty or more feet from the building itself when he saw the sunlight flash on something embedded between the tar and a cement parking abutment. "Ralph, get over here!" Harry was already stooping over when Ralph came to his side.

"What is it, Harry, what did you find?"

"Let's have that bag, constable. What we've got is about the best piece of evidence yet." He wondered to himself why the CID had missed it. Harry dug the lead up with his knife, using his handkerchief to lift it and dropped it into the bag. "Ralph, I'm taking you back to your car. You'll be going to the barrens alone. I'll fill you in as I drive."

—

Pat and Marge had spent the last several days together doing what they both loved most: fishing and hunting, although neither were in season. Their freezer was full of the late summer catches of eel and several other species of fish, along with another recently butchered deer. The two women sat on the front step of the cabin. Pat was sipping on a freshly brewed cup of coffee, and Marge chattered on about her ability with her 30/30 while clouds of smoke billowed from her corncob pipe. Pat felt good about her decision several days earlier to question Marge calmly as to her whereabouts on Friday night, and was reassured that Marge was not capable of killing anyone. Certainly, she was a high-strung person, a very strong personality, which most people did not understand. Although in her heart Pat knew that eventually she would no longer be able to shy away from Jimmy and their destiny, for now she thought he understood. Marge was as important to Pat as she was to Marge, but Pat, right now, was the only one who knew why.

Marge broke the silence. "Well, little Pat, I was thinking."

"Oh, I hate it when you say that," responded Pat. Both women chuckled.

"Well, I think we have room for one more deer in that freezer."

"Oh, you do?"

"Yes, I do little Pat, I think if we went out, oh maybe tonight, we ought to have enough meat to last 'til at least mid-hunting season." It was good to hear Marge's old self, but would it last? Lately, it seemed there was always something touching her off.

Pat knew she must do her best to stay with her as much as possible until she was completely sure Marge was regaining her self-confidence. "Don't you think we'd be pressing our luck by going back out tonight?"

"No, I don't, little Pat, no, I don't."

"Well, why don't we see how things look toward the end of the day, and if we can work it in, why don't we go ahead?"

"I don't know what I'd do without you, little Pat, I really don't." Pat smiled and sipped once more on the coffee as Marge walked away, half-puffing on the pipe and half-muttering to Pat as she went.

Later, with Marge clanking around in the shed, tinkering with some trivial pursuit, Pat was alone with her thoughts. *"Jimmy White was naked on her bed, and she was standing over him in a white see-through top, inviting him to have his way with her."* She needed him, now more than ever. She longed for his touch, wanted their lips together, she wanted to be held by his strong arms. Her eyes were closed, the sun warm on her face. She whispered, "I love you, Jimmy." She never realized that Marge had come out of the shed. Marge's voice broke the silence. "What did you say, little Pat? Were you saying something to me?" Pat exhaled quietly, trying desperately to hide her true feelings of having such a terrific daydream shattered by the sound of Marge's voice. "No dea', I wasn't talking to you." She was being sarcastic by stressing the word, dea'.

"I know," responded Marge in a sing-song voice, "you were talking to your sweetheart, Jimmy, bubba and didn't think I could hear you."

Suddenly, Pat saw the humor in all of it and they both broke out into laughter.

—

With his new piece of evidence in hand, Harry wasted little time leaving for the crime lab. The distance between places in Washington County was always a factor concerning any investigation, regardless of its severity. He thought to himself, *"This will probably turn out to be another long day without Annie."* He looked at his watch: 8:40 a.m. He was getting off at the Augusta exit. "Ha, that's damn good time. I get this wrapped up here; I'll still have time to question Davis again before supper."

As he eased the vehicle off the ramp, he squeezed in behind a twenty-two-wheel logging truck, and settled in. The length of the line in front of him indicated it would be a slow ride through the capitol. He wondered now if he'd told Ralph everything he wanted him to look for out on the barrens; if he hadn't, for the life of him he couldn't think of it now. He thought to call Annie before leaving the capitol; then hoped he wouldn't forget.

His mind raced with new questions. So far, everything seemed fine. The bullet had entered the head and exited—he'd found it. Davis had said he was already dead; he didn't kill him. Who did? Irene? Harry had known for some time of Lester and Irene's involvement, but never really wanted to know details. Now he would have to know. He was surprised that Irene and Davis had once been involved. Depending on his time and how much of it he'd spend with Davis later today, he might be able to get to Irene. She would have to be questioned. She was involved with both men, one of which had been brutally murdered, the other desecrated the body. This was the part of his job he loved the most: putting all of the pieces together, building the case, finding the guilty, and finally, judgment day!

—

Ralph diligently executed his assignment on the barrens. He followed every instruction Harry gave him, but found nothing. The constable was always insecure and unsure when dealing with

Harry and his unpredictable moods, and felt a hollowness deep within him. Ralph spoke softly to himself as he walked the several yards toward his cruiser. "I hope he doesn't embarrass me in front of anyone, that's all."

—

Harry arrived at the Crime Lab sooner than he'd anticipated. The traffic had moved steadily, and there'd been no snarls at the rotary. He went in through the rear entrance, a metal-framed glass enclosure that faced the capitol building with its towering granite rotunda and green dome, overlooking the steep banks of the Kennebec River. He walked briskly through the narrow corridor to the lab itself, nodding occasionally to the white-lab-coat-clad technicians who offered their good morning greeting. He singled out the lab tech he knew had been working on this particular case, and moved toward him like a predator after prey.

"Well, well, hard at work on my case, I hope?" Harry asked flippantly.

Somewhat surprised, the lab tech looked up from the microscope, cross-eyed and straining, trying to focus his vision. "Christ, almighty," Harry laughed. "Don't you know you're supposed to give your eyes a breather once in a while?"

Eyes focused now, the technician coughed a slight laugh and responded. "I'm just glad I was working instead of having a cup of coffee when you walked through the door. As you already know, he was killed by the bullet through the head, which entered just behind the left ear, and exited just above the right eyebrow."

Upon hearing that, Harry flipped the baggy containing the damaged piece of lead onto the table. "How long will it take you to find out if this made the hole?" Harry smiled as the young tech lifted the baggie and examined the contents.

"Give me about an hour. Get some coffee; I'll give you everything as soon as I'm done."

"Fine," Harry said. He wasted little time finding the coffee pot, and then found an empty office and a telephone. He dialed his home number, and hoped Annie was still there.

"Hello," the soft voice answered.

"Hello, yourself," Harry responded.

"Where are you?"

"I'm in Augusta."

"How are things going?"

"Not too bad, Annie. I should be out of here in a reasonable amount of time."

"That's great, how are you holding up? You haven't been getting all that much sleep lately."

"Well, I'm doing okay, really. Thank God for caffeine. Have you been over to see Betty?"

"No, I haven't. I've been waiting to see if you'd call."

"You're sweet. When this is all over, what do you say to an evening at our favorite Italian restaurant and a movie in Bangor?"

"You'd better believe it. I'll hold you to that, Harry." The conversation went back and forth for some time, giving each of them what they longed for most—each other—even if it was over the telephone. Harry lost track of time.

Through the opened door, he saw the technician stride past. Harry laughed because the young man's appearance was the epitome of a nutty professor in his long, white lab coat and distressed face. Harry blanketed the mouthpiece of the phone and called out, "Hey, professor, I'm in here." Then he went back to say his good-byes to Annie. He was just placing the receiver into the cradle when the young man appeared at the door.

"Got it for you, Harry! .30-caliber, everything fits."

"Could you tell if it came from a pistol or a rifle?"

"I'd say it came from a small automatic-type pistol." In his right hand, the technician held, with some apparent fondness, a steaming cup of coffee, in his left, a large manila envelope.

"Is everything I need in that envelope?" Harry asked.

"Yes, it sure is."

"Good, then I'll be on my way Down East."

"Say, I've been thinking about heading down your way this fall—maybe I'll look you up, Harry."

"Yah, you do that," Harry exclaimed, thinking the young man was merely making conversation. Harry walked quickly through the building, avoiding eye contact with anyone who could slow his pace or distract him from his departure. He slid in behind the wheel of his car, and in seconds the vehicle was moving toward the exit. The mid-morning traffic was calm, and he maneuvered his vehicle through several quick turns that avoided the downtown area. Taking the on ramp of the interstate, he put his foot to the floor.

His blue car pulled into the driveway two hours from the time he'd hit I-95. He saw Annie looking through the kitchen window with that school-girl happy look she was readily able to display without notice. He got out of the car and went in through the kitchen door. "Hi," it's good to see you."

"Mm, it's good to see you too," she responded as they embraced. "Are you staying home tonight?"

"I thought I might have some lunch, if you could fix it."

"No problem, anything special?"

"Anything will be fine, Annie." Harry walked into the living room and sat himself heavily on the sofa, wishing the case were solved right now. He lifted and pinched the two metal tabs that held the flap on the envelope closed, reached in, and pulled the report out. Harry read it carefully, eyeing his notes occasionally. Annie brought a sandwich, a cup of coffee, and a kiss, and then left him alone. He remained on the sofa, nibbling the sandwich and sipping the coffee. Annie made no attempt to interrupt. She merely refilled the cup when she noticed it was empty. He'd remained in his place for well over an hour when finally he inhaled a large breath and stretched as he exhaled. "Done!" he exclaimed.

"Does everything fit into place?" Annie asked from the kitchen.

"Well, as far as I can see, it all seems to fit so far, but if what Davis said is true, someone in this town is a murderer."

"My God. Have you any suspects?"

"I really shouldn't discuss it right now, not until I question Davis again."

"So, you'll be going back to the jail today?"

"The sooner I get there, the sooner I'll get back here to my favorite girlfriend."

"Your only girlfriend, you mean."

"Yeah, of course," he said with a smile. "Oh, did Ralph call?"

"No, I've been here all day, and you're the only one who's called." Harry reached for the telephone and dialed. He looked toward Annie, who'd been looking directly at him since he'd made the comment about the girlfriend and told her he loved her. Her eyes grew as she expressed her need for more. Harry immediately picked up on it, and was about to comment when the line became open.

"Ralph Bailey here!"

"Constable, what the hell are you doing home in the middle of the afternoon during a murder investigation?"

Ralph's stutter came over the phone as he searched for words, but nothing but babble came out.

"Never mind," Harry said. "Did you find anything on the barrens?"

"Nothing, Harry, except those same tire tracks across that

second-year burn."

"Ya, well, we had to make sure. You want to come out to Machias with me and question Davis?" Ralph seemed surprised at the invitation. Harry was asking him to go along to question a suspect. "Well, are ya' coming or not?"

"Yes, yes, I'll go, Harry."

"Fine, I'll pick you up in about ten minutes."

"Fine, Harry, I'll be ready." Each man hung up simultaneously.

Annie smirked at Harry. "So, shall I have the bath water hot when you come home?" He smiled a dirty little grin, and merely nodded his head in approval.

—

Davis was escorted into the small room by a county deputy. Harry and Ralph were already seated at the large table in the center of the room, positioned so they would be facing Davis as he entered. Davis remained standing, starring at the two men seated before him.

"Sit down, Davis." Harry ordered.

Davis walked to the single chair on his side of the table. He looked at Ralph, and said, "I'm sorry for shooting at you. I hope you weren't hurt."

"No, I'm fine Davis, but I can't say the same for my cruiser."

"Oh ya, I do remember seeing a bunch of glass flying around and I..."

Harry interrupted, "I need to ask some more questions, if it's all right with you, Constable?"

"Yeah, sure, Harry, go ahead." Harry turned toward the constable with a look that said, "You've got to be kidding." Ralph's face became pale as he focused his stare in Davis's direction.

"You told me you found Lester near the drive-up window," Harry stated.

"That's right."

"How close?"

"I don't remember exactly."

Harry raised his voice slightly. "Was it ten, twelve, twenty feet, what?"

"I don't remember exactly, what do you want me to say?"

"Were you carrying a firearm with you on Friday night?"

"I had a couple with me."

"So, what did you have?"

"I had my Winchester 30/30, and my old .38 pistol." Harry's stare was cold and penetrating. "I told you I didn't kill him." Without blinking, Harry's thoughts went back to earlier at the crime lab and the lab tech's comment: *"I'd say it came from a small automatic-type pistol, .30-caliber; everything fits."* Davis continued his stare as he lit a cigarette.

Harry spoke. "Did you fire either weapon during the course of the day?"

"Shot a few bottles with the .38 is all."

"What about the 30/30?"

"Nope...I never even loaded it."

"You have to know Davis, that each and every one of your firearms have been confiscated and will be fired for ballistics."

Davis drew deeply on the cigarette and as he was about to exhale, he looked toward Ralph with a half-grin, then slowly turned toward Harry and said, "I don't give a fuck!"

Harry was visibly irritated. "If it takes me a month to get every answer that I want from you, I'll let you rot here." Ralph's eyes moved rapidly between the two men. He'd never seen Harry so red in the face or so close to losing control.

"Look," Davis responded, "I told you everything when you first questioned me. Nothin's changed."

"Let's start over," Harry said. "You came to, got out of your truck, and on your return to the cab, you saw the body."

"Right!"

"You went over to see, and realized it was Lester."

"Right!"

"Then you laughed."

"Right!"

"You picked him up, dragged him to the truck and lifted him into the back, but weren't sure what you'd do with him yet."

"Right!"

"But, after a few drinks, you figured it out."

"Right!"

"You tied the poor man to the rack and you gutted him!"

"Right!…right!…right!" Davis shouted.

Davis was not about to change his story. Harry however, was allowing his personal feelings to overshadow his impartiality. He also knew the contents of the ballistics report, and unless something drastic changed, the police had nothing. Harry sat quietly for several minutes pretending to read from the report. Both Ralph Bailey and Davis Norton appeared confused at Harry's silence, yet neither man attempted to speak.

Harry looked up then, looked around the room. "Could you guys use a coffee?" Both men were surprised at the question, and merely nodded to indicate they could.

"Fine," Harry said, "Ralph, you stay here and keep Davis company for a minute. I'll get the coffee." Both men's eyes remained locked on each other as Harry walked out. His soft-soled shoes made no sound through the empty hall.

A feeling of complete consternation filled his entire consciousness. *"Okay, okay,"* he thought, *"live with it, Davis isn't the killer. He found the body, wanted to get even, that was his way. That leaves Irene, or does it? Why would Irene kill her lover? They had a fight… too easy. He bid her adios, maybe. Why not, he was sleeping with Betty the night he left and was murdered."* The day of the funeral came back, along with his promise: *"I will leave no stone unturned."*

—

Upon his return, the three men sat and drank their coffee in silence. Davis drew heavily from his cigarette between gulps. Ralph seemed composed, pushed back on the two rear legs of the old metal chair. Harry, deep in thought, contemplated what he'd say next. Suddenly he spoke up, "Davis, did you kill Lester Sawyer?"

"No, I did not!"

"Do you know who did?" And as the words left his lips, he realized the futility of the question.

"No, I don't!" was Davis's reply.

"You'll be seeing the judge in the morning." Harry stood up and went to the door, then stopped. He turned slowly and faced Davis. "I want you to know, Davis, that I believe what you've told me. But it won't be up to me to decide. I'll continue digging, and if I find something, you'd better believe I'll be back."

## CHAPTER 10

LIFE SLOWLY RETURNED TO NORMAL in the small town by the river now that Lester Sawyer's funeral was over. The excitement of the shoot-out and police stand-off with Davis Norton died down. All that seemed left was an occasional rumor and a few whispers at the Quick-Stop. A lull fell over the area, one that separated the seasonal onslaught of tourists in their so-called large traveling toilets and the sport-car, binocular-clad leaf-peepers of fall. A lull, welcomed by a large percentage of everyday Joes, yet loathed by the small business community. It was however, business as usual for Harry Circus, Maine State Trooper assigned to Berryville, Maine.

It was rare when a case of this magnitude developed in any of the small communities. The last murder investigation had been conducted by the now-retired trooper, Morry, who had supervised Harry when Harry first joined the State Police. That investigation was Morry's responsibility. This investigation was Harry's and it was becoming his entire life.

He arose every morning thinking of it, had it with coffee all day, breathed it with dinner each night, and lived it to a point of near-total neglect of his life with Annie.

It didn't seem so long ago that the thought of anything coming between Annie and her man could have ever entered her consciousness, yet now it was becoming a very real part of her everyday life. She wanted it all to go away, all of it. No more calls from the Criminal Investigation Division, no more reports with lunch, no more middle-of-the-night phone calls, no more trips to Augusta, no more Tim Barnes. She wanted her husband back, all of him. She would not be plagued by guilt because of the way she now felt, however, she knew and loved her husband with all of her heart. She knew how important the entire investigation was to Harry, and as it was and always would be, Annie was standing by her man.

—

10:30 a.m.: What should have been a leisurely Saturday now found Harry Circus speeding to the questioning of a surprise suspect. An anonymous caller had asked for Harry soon after his arrival at headquarters. Through the receiver, the voice seemed vaguely familiar, yet muffled enough to make identification impossible. The caller had told Harry that on the Friday evening of Lester Sawyer's murder, they had observed Marge, walking in the field behind the bank carrying a rifle. The one person who Harry considered a most volatile personality had been overlooked completely in all of the searching of his notes and records.

The roar of the equipment-laden trooper car was heavy on the black-top as it sped toward Berryville. In his mind, Harry tried to convince himself of a motive. *"Why would Marge kill Lester? She was prone to violence, but murder?"* Thinking back on his original talk with Betty, he recalled her telling him about the early morning phone call. "*If it was Marge, where did she call from?*" No problem, he thought, "*pay phone at the Quick-Stop. It's within walking distance to the bank.*"

Harry turned onto the gravel way that led to Marge's cabin. The dust from his tires billowed high above the car, encapsulating the entire road. The sound of the rapidly approaching vehicle gave both women a start. Pat stood erect, facial expression held in a defiant stare as if to challenge the trooper's presence. Marge stood at the entrance to the shed where she'd been tinkering, eyes wide, the fear obvious on her face.

Harry brought the vehicle to a stop directly in front of Pat, swinging the door open and leaving it in that position. "I need to talk to Marge!"

"Oh, what about?" Pat asked. A cold shiver raced from the base of her spine to the back of her skull at Harry's response.

"I'd like to know where she was the night of the VFW dance. The same night Lester Sawyer was murdered."

"You have to be kidding me!"

"It's no kidding matter. Now we can do this here, or we can go to Machias." Pat continued staring at Harry. Marge had not moved a muscle, nor had she changed her facial expression. Pat turned and motioned for Marge to come. Hesitantly, she moved slowly toward them. "Can we go inside?" Harry asked.

"No," Pat responded abruptly. "You want to ask her some questions, you ask 'em' right here!"

"First, I'm going to ask you a question, Pat. Were you at that dance?"

"Yes, I was. Why?"

"Who was with you?"

"I thought you wanted to talk to Marge, Harry?"

"Look, Harry said, "what I want is a little cooperation. I can get it here or…"

Pat interrupted him. "I was with Jimmy White." Harry wrote it down in his notebook. "What time did you get home?"

"Just after midnight."

"Was Marge here?" Pat stood silent, unable to speak, her thoughts going back to that Friday evening upon returning to the cabin with Jimmy and finding it empty.

"Well, was she here or not?"

"No!" was all that Pat could respond.

Harry turned to Marge. "So, where were you, Marge?" She stood looking at the ground as if the very earth beneath her feet would speak for her.

"Marge, I'm asking you a question." Still, she stood silent, unable to speak.

Pat moved slowly toward her, placing her hand gently on one of her shoulders. "Marge. Marge, you've got to give Harry an answer, please." Marge looked up slowly staring at Pat through deeply bewildered eyes, but said absolutely nothing. All three stood silently for what seemed an eternity. The breezes blowing through the tall pines that surrounded the entire area engulfed them in an eerie whistling.

"I'm going to have to take her into custody if she doesn't talk to me."

"Please, Marge," Pat asked desperately, "answer Harry's question. Where were you on that Friday night?" Marge remained silent.

"Marge, you'll have to come with me." Harry walked toward her, placing his hands around her left forearm, tugging her gently toward the waiting blue car.

"Christ, Harry, there must be something else you can do besides arresting her. You can't really believe she had anything to do with that murder."

"I'm not arresting her. She'll be detained in Machias for more questioning. I received a call about an hour ago that puts her behind the bank that Saturday in the early morning."

"Early morning…what? Ten…eleven a.m.?" Pat asked.

"Middle of the night, early morning," responded Harry. He ran his hands slowly around Marge's waist and down her pant legs around the ankles, staying well away from any part of her body that could later be considered an improper search. He placed the handcuffs on loosely, and assisted her into the rear seat. Upon closing the rear door, he turned to Pat and asked, "Does Marge own a 30/30 rifle or .30 caliber pistol?"

"She has a 30/30. Why? You have nothing on her. She couldn't kill anyone."

"Why won't she answer my question, then?"

"Look, Harry, leave her with me for a couple of hours. I'll get her to talk for you."

"I don't have a couple of hours, Pat. You want to talk to her, follow us to Machias."

"You don't know what you're doing. This is going to mess her up bad."

As Harry slid behind the wheel, he turned to Pat. "If you have anything I can use, you'd better tell me." He waited for a moment, and when Pat didn't respond, he slammed the door and pulled away, leaving Pat in a thick, dusty cloud, feeling a sensation of impending doom.

Pat sat on the front step to the cabin and began to weep, her elbows planted in her lap, her open hands supporting her head. Tears flowed freely between her fingers and down the backs of her hands. Her emotions were mixed with sorrow and anger—the sorrow of having to watch Marge taken by the trooper, a person she knew could no more have killed a man than she herself could have, and anger at the man who took her because he didn't have the time to wait.

"What I am going to do?" Pat whispered to herself, but her mind was a blank. She knew one thing. Marge would need her, now more than ever. *"Jimmy!"* she cried in her mind, and immediately stood, running toward the old Wagoneer. She had to be with him. He'd be the only one to understand. No one could support her like he would.

## CHAPTER 11

IRENE AWOKE FEELING THE EFFECTS of another evening spent with old movies and Scotch on the rocks. Her face was beginning to show the effects of the past week of mourning, drinking, chain-smoking and crying following the murder and funeral of her lover, Lester Sawyer. She hadn't raised a shade nor opened a blind in over a week. She had no intention of returning to the bank. Her accrued vacation time and sick leave would give her in the neighborhood of six weeks off, of which she intended to use every minute. The answering machine was used to screen every call, and since the beginning of her self-imposed seclusion, she had answered only one caller, Harry Circus. He'd called several days earlier, and since this was Saturday, she doubted he'd be here today. In her mind, she knew what Harry wanted to know, and thought perhaps he already knew.

Harry arrived at the county jail about thirty-five minutes after leaving Berryville. During their short trip he tried several times to get Marge to talk, but to no avail. Marge simply would not communicate. As they walked in through the rear entrance, he informed the guard that she was being brought in for questioning, and because of special circumstances, her close friend Pat must be allowed to see her, if and when she arrived. Then he looked at Marge. "Pat will be here soon. I want you to think about what I asked you earlier. Do you understand, Marge?" Marge continued looking down at the floor. She gave absolutely no indication that she even heard what Harry said.

Harry shook his head in disbelief as the guard escorted her down the narrow corridor to a small questioning room. Harry sat at a small corner desk, looking over his notes. He knew first thing Monday morning a judge would probably decide to have Davis Norton sent to Bangor Mental Health Institute for psychiatric evaluation, and right now, Harry believed Davis was a wacko. He was convinced that what Davis had confessed to was in actuality the extent of his involvement with the murder. He couldn't be sure how things would go with Marge.

Irene was the next person to be questioned. That would be today, and then Betty Sawyer. Harry sat back in his chair and wondered how Betty was holding up. The stand-off with Davis, the ensuing questioning, and trips to the crime lab had made it impossible for him to see Betty since the morning the body had been found on the barrens. "Oh, so many things to do," he said, the words so soft that only he could hear.

Harry looked down the long narrow corridor with its high ceilings and white concrete-block walls. The floors were always shining and clean, as was the entire building, but he could not help notice how the pungent smell of an institutional atmosphere grabbed at your nostrils as you walked through the doors. He pictured in his mind how many times he'd escorted prisoners through these halls. Some—the least violent—walked calmly without trouble, but the others—the big, tough guys, the ones that deserved to be here—usually had to be dragged, sometimes kicking and screaming all the way to their cells like little children brought to their rooms by an angry parent.

"Chicken-shit little punks," Harry whispered to himself as he bent over his notes, jotting down what he'd ask Irene later. He was about to place his notebook into his shirt pocket when a guard approached from the far end of the hallway. Harry sat silently watching the guard as he came nearer.

"Trooper Circus, there are two people out in the visitor's entrance. The woman said you told her she could see Marge as soon as they arrived."

"Oh, yeah," replied Harry. "I didn't think she'd get here this fast." Harry stood immediately and accompanied the guard to the front of the building. As he walked through the reception office with its reinforced glass facade, he was surprised at seeing Jimmy White as the person who'd accompanied Pat to the jail. When he reached the door, his attention was diverted by the buzzing sound of the electrically activated lock release. He turned toward the female guard who was seated at the control panel and who'd activated the release, thanking her as he walked out into the lobby.

He greeted Jimmy with a dry quip. "You do know that the speed limit between Berryville and Machias is posted at fifty." Neither Pat nor Jimmy responded, nor even seemed amused by the trooper's humor. Harry became instantly straight-faced and began speaking. "Pat, I really hope you can get her to cooperate with me. She could be in a lot of trouble."

Pat responded with a somewhat agitated tone. "You know damned well you could have waited twenty minutes. I could have gotten her to open up enough for you to get what you needed out of her."

"Look," answered Harry, "I've been working around the clock on this case since the very first minute. I've offered everyone concerned every opportunity that my patience will allow. I'm not going to stand around in someone's dooryard on a Saturday morning while they look to the ground for some mystical revelation."

"You don't need to be this cold toward her. You know very well what her situation is, and you have nothing but time." Harry and Pat stood silently facing each other, each having much more they could have added, but their facial expressions seemed to indicate an inevitable stalemate. Harry turned and walked to the reception window asking that Marge be brought to the visitor's station. He turned, telling them that Pat would be the only one allowed in. Pat stood silently facing the cold, gray, windowless metal door that would lead to the visitor's area. In her mind, she could not imagine how she would begin to converse with Marge.

Pat seemed startled at the buzzing of the electrically activated door and the voice of the female guard over the speaker telling her to go ahead through to the visitor room. Jimmy was not allowed to go with her. It was a short walk to the questioning room. Pat sat quietly, waiting for Marge to be brought in. She felt uncomfortable, as if she were being watched. She heard the closing sounds of several doors, then footsteps. Soon, Marge, accompanied by a young-looking jail guard, came through the door opposite the glass divider. The guard led her to the chair across from Pat, then left.

Pat waited until the door was completely closed before she began speaking. "Are you all right, Marge?" Marge gave no response. "Marge, it's okay, they can't hear us here, and you have to let me help you. I can get you out, but you have to talk to me. Please Marge!" It was quiet for a moment as both women sat looking at each other. Pat's thoughts went back over the last several days—it seemed that everything was getting back to normal between them. It wasn't fair. Their life was always so full of shit, one thing after another. When the hell would it all end? When would she ever see her life take on some normalcy?

Suddenly, Marge spoke. "Why am I here, little Pat?"

"You're here because you wouldn't answer Harry's questions."

"Oh, yeah, I remember now. He wanted to know where I was last Friday night."

"That's right; now why don't you talk to me for a while? Let's just relax a little."

"Okay," responded Marge, "what do you want to talk about, little Pat?"

"Well, for starters, how in hell are you going to make it in here? They don't allow smoking." With that said, Marge displayed a totally annoyed look.

Harry remained in the glassed-in reception office, shooting the breeze with one of the guards who shared an enthusiasm for fishing. The small talk seemed to calm the trooper from the insurmountable stress. Several times during the conversation, Harry's mind seemed to leave his very consciousness, taking him on an excursion to the icy blue waters of a secluded lake far to the north that he loved. It was rare to find another angler, casting to the same rhythm of the wind-blown swells tapping against the bow. Now he wanted his life back, all of it. He thought to himself as the guard continued talking, *"I will go fishing after this thing is over."*

Just then, the buzzer sounded and a voice crackled over the speaker. It was Pat's voice. Harry took what appeared to be two giant steps toward the control panel where the female guard was seated, and asked whose responsibility it was to maintain contact orally and visually with guards, prisoners, and visitors throughout the facility. Displaying a look that might suggest annoyance, the guard immediately depressed the speak button in front of her, asking Pat, "Is everything all right down there?"

Pat spoke once more. "Is Harry Circus still here? I think we'd like to speak with him now." Without saying a word, Harry went immediately to the door. The guard, anticipating his walking speed, activated the lock release before he even touched the doorknob.

Harry had no idea what to expect from Marge. He knew she was unstable, but he really did not know her as a person. Whether or not she was capable of murder, he really couldn't tell, but whatever it was they were ready to talk about, he hoped it would bring him one step closer to solving this case.

Harry quickly traveled the short distance between the control room and the visitor's station. He went directly to the visitor section where Pat was seated. The younger guard went to the prisoner side to escort Marge to a more private questioning room. When they arrived, Harry motioned for both women to be seated at the side of the table opposite the door. He sat with his back to the door. He told the guard that everything would be fine, and asked if he would wait out in the hall. The guard closed the door on his way out.

"Well, girls, can I assume that everything has gone all right in here?"

"Let's just say it went," responded Pat.

"Is she prepared to answer my questions?"

"Why don't you ask some and see, Harry?"

"All right, but before I do that I'm going to read her, her rights." When he finished, he asked Marge if she understood. Pat, assuming that everything would go well, suddenly became weak with disbelief when Marge refused to speak.

"I don't believe this! Pat, what the hell is going on here?" Harry asked.

"Marge, don't do this!" Pat cried. "We all want the same thing here. I want to take you home with me, but I can't do that unless you cooperate with Harry." Marge, with her hands resting on the table in front of her, fingers entwined as if engulfed in prayer, remained silent.

Harry got up and strode to the door. Pat followed. "Look Pat," Harry said, "why don't I get us some coffee, and you go back in there and try and reassure her. We'll start fresh when I get back." Pat nodded in agreement, then went back into the room.

*CHAPTER 12*

---

MARGE WAS SEATED ON THE CHAIR; her knees were drawn tight to her chest and held by her encircling arms. The expression on her face revealed a withdrawn, depressed demeanor. Pat was seated across from her in quiet dismay. Marge's position was unchanged when she began speaking, taking Pat completely off guard. "I didn't kill that son of a bitch, little Pat, I didn't do it." Pat's jaw dropped, leaving her mouth agape.

"What did you say?" A smile slowly appeared on her face.

"I said I didn't kill 'im!"

Pat breathed a sigh of relief. "Why has it taken you so long to say it?"

"Because I hate that goddamned Harry Circus, and he thought I did it. I hate Harry Circus." As the words left her mouth, both women were startled by the sudden appearance of a figure at the door. It was Harry Circus.

"Well, ladies, it seems as though I'm right on time. Was that just girl talk, or did I overhear a declaration of innocence?" Marge had assumed an erect posture, and was staring directly at Pat, eyes enlarged with fear.

"What you heard just now, you've known to be the truth. You wanted her to say it," replied Pat.

"We all have our responsibilities. Now if we can just wrap this up with a few short questions, I'll see to it you're out of here within the hour."

Pat looked to Marge for a reaction, but saw only a skeptical expression. "Marge, are you ready to work with me on this?" Marge said nothing. She simply nodded her head, indicating she would.

—

At approximately the very moment that Harry began taking Marge's statement, a telephone call was being placed to the district attorney's private phone. Lab tests performed on a knife taken from Davis Norton's home confirmed through blood analysis that it had been the very knife used in the disembowelment of Lester Sawyer. That, along with two near-perfect fingerprints belonging to Davis, confirmed his involvement beyond a shadow of a doubt. Along with these findings, the long-awaited report on the shattered glass found in the bank's rear parking lot showed trace amounts of Lester's blood, and was found to be from a late-model mid-sized Ford vehicle.

—

Harry looked at his watch, and immediately began questioning Marge. "Why don't we start with the first thing on my mind? Did you kill Lester Sawyer?"

Marge looked Harry right in the eye. "No, I didn't!"

"Do you know who did?"

"No, I don't!" Harry appeared bewildered, but moved quickly to the next question. "Were you near the bank the night Lester Sawyer was murdered?"

Harry immediately remembered the anonymous call telling him that she was. Marge seemed afraid now, and began to slip into what appeared to be her usual trance to avoid the question. "Marge," Harry said austerely, "Don't slip away from me now!"

Pat slid forward on her chair, calling out "Marge! Marge!" The second call brought her head up.

She looked at Pat, eyes wide and alert, responding, "Yes!"

Both Harry and Pat raised their eyebrows simultaneously. Harry, visibly pleased, said, "Now we're getting somewhere." Pat, knowing very well the speed at which Marge could withdraw from any situation, looked toward Harry.

"I wouldn't rush this if I were you." Harry jerked quickly in Pat's direction, and was about to return a defiant remark when suddenly, as if reading Pat's mind, he remained silent and looked toward Marge. He saw that she was very close to slipping away.

"Relax," Harry said softly, "don't get nervous. I believe what you've told me so far. I just need a little more help." Harry stood, asking Pat to follow him out of the room. Pat stood, reassuring Marge that she would only be a moment, and went outside with Harry.

"Look, Pat, I'm going to be as easy with her as I possibly can. She's a free girl as soon as we wrap this up. I believe what she's telling me, but I think she's holding back for some reason." Pat agreed that Marge was holding something back, and said she would help in any way she could, returning inside while Harry took a breather.

He walked slowly through the narrow hall. The sound of his soft-soled shoes squeaked out an echo that trailed him. His mind raced with the thoughts of the investigation and his return momentarily to the questioning. There was something out of sync with all of this, and it made Harry very uncomfortable. He walked the halls for about ten minutes, and upon returning to the room, Harry stood quietly at the sight of the two women embracing. Both were in tears, yet both were smiling. Pat was speaking mellifluously. He entered the room and sat himself quietly in his chair.

Harry was running out of time. He couldn't hold Marge for more than a few hours, and he knew it. He began with Pat's signal.

"Marge, a little while ago, you told me that you were near the bank the night Lester was murdered." Marge nodded in agreement. "Now, this morning when I asked Pat if you were at home when she returned from the dance, she told me no." He paused. "Don't you think that was a little late for you to be outside by yourself?" Marge hesitated a moment, then nodded her head in agreement. Harry paused once again to give her space and then began again. "Marge, I want you to take a deep breath, relax and tell Pat and me everything you did from the time you left the cabin until the time you came home that evening. I promise you won't get into trouble if you tell us the truth. We need your help, Marge."

She looked toward Pat, then back at Harry, and began a verbose account of her whereabouts that evening. Harry wrote as fast as his fingers could push the pen, but it was impossible to get every word. He concentrated only on what he believed was pertinent. Both Pat and Harry stopped her along the way so that she might clarify a certain incident or give a more detailed explanation of a statement. Nothing of what Marge said seemed to trigger any interest in the trooper until she indicated her return to the cabin to get her 30/30.

"Why did you think you needed your rifle?" he asked.

"Well, it was late and you never know—you could run into a

bear, you know. They roam around at night."

"That's true," replied Harry, "but is that the only reason you went back for your rifle?" Marge froze, looking directly at Pat, eyes large and unblinking.

"Marge," Harry said soothingly, "everything will be fine if you tell me the truth." Pat nodded her head as if to indicate that all would be fine, prompting Marge to continue.

"Well...I chased a couple of raccoons up a tree on the other side of the big field behind the bank."

"Go on," Harry said.

"I shot 'em both, all right! I shot 'em both right in the head. I killed 'em, I killed 'em!" The intensity with which Marge now spoke forced Harry to put his pen down, bringing him to a straight, rigid posture in his chair. Pat stood, going directly to Marge's side and placing her arm around her shoulder consolingly. Harry sat motionless, staring at the two women. He knew in his mind that he couldn't rush this, and the longer he looked at Marge, the more he wondered at the complexities of this woman. He now recalled his promise at the cemetery. *"I will leave no stone unturned."*

Pat turned facing Harry, and said, "She's ready." Harry cleared his throat and started again.

"Marge, do you know about what time it was when you got back to the other side of the field and shot the raccoons?" Marge simply shook her head no. Pat suddenly realized what Marge had meant upon returning to the cabin that night when she said to Jimmy, "I'll kill you next, you bastard," a statement she hoped Marge would not remember.

"All right," Harry said, "what happened next?"

Marge thought for a moment and with a facial expression as serious as a heart attack she said. "Well, both o' them fuckers fell right out o' that tree." Marge's face remained as serious as a priest's in a pulpit. It took all that Harry had to keep a straight face; however, that was not the case for Pat as she burst forth in laughter, Marge joining her. Harry couldn't help wondering, watching the two women frolicking at the statement how two people their age could be so nonchalant at such a serious time. He expressed his dissatisfaction with a cold, unmoving stare in their direction, bringing them both to a sudden, intense seriousness and quiet. "May we proceed, please?" Harry asked sternly.

His voice now bordered on sarcasm. "What did you do next?"

Marge spoke in a low voice. "Well, I covered them coons with leaves so I could come back later and get 'em, then I left."

Quickly, Harry asked, "Which way did you go?" Marge's sudden response took Pat and the trooper completely by surprise.

"I didn't shoot 'im! I don't own a gun like that!" Harry seemed riveted to the spot, but realizing he must continue, spoke quickly.

"Did you see Lester Sawyer get shot?"

"Yes, I did! Yes, I did!" Marge began shaking uncontrollably. Pat again went quickly to her side, remaining with her as another question was fired from the trooper's mouth.

"Where were you exactly when you saw the shooting?"

"I was standing at the edge of the parking lot. It was too dark, no one could see me. I was scared. I thought someone was shooting at me!" Pat held her tight. It was important now for Harry to preserve her trust. He looked to Pat for reassurance, and as their eyes met, he felt her approval to continue. "Marge, are you all right?" he asked.

A moment passed before she responded.

"Yes!"

"We're almost there. You'll be going home soon." With that, both women looked at each other and smiled faintly.

"Let's just run over this a little, Marge. You came out of the field and saw a car near the bank."

"No," responded Marge, "when I got to the edge of the parking lot, that's when I heard the shot, then the glass broke. I ducked, and then I saw the car." Harry was relieved that she was able to relate the events to him in her own way.

"Go ahead, Marge. Tell me the rest of what you saw."

With Pat at her side, Marge's face now seemed to radiate self-confidence. "I was scared!" Her head shook, her eyes enlarged with intensity. "I was scared! I didn't move an inch. The door of the car opened, and he fell out. I saw his bald head bounce on the ground. He was all bloody." Her voice increased in volume. Pat was rubbing her shoulders. "In a couple of seconds, I think, the car drove away real fast. I ran away, no one saw me. I went home!"

Harry's notepad seemed to be filling quickly. Unconcerned, he continued writing. He looked up. "Marge, did you see who was driving that car?"

"Well, I saw the person, but I don't know who it was. They were wearing a big hat."

"A big hat?" Harry asked. "What kind of a big hat?"

"A big hat! A big hat! Aaaa...cowboy hat, that's what it was, a cowboy hat." Marge seemed totally pleased with herself. Pat hugged her, telling her how pleased she was and how much of a help she was being.

Harry's voice was calm as he asked the next question. "Marge, what color was the car?"

Quickly Marge responded, "White!"

"How many doors did it have?"

"Four!"

"Do you know what kind of car it was?" Harry was searching; however, what Marge now offered would help, if only slightly.

"Well, it was smaller than Lester's. I think it was Lester's that was parked behind it and it was smaller."

"Can you tell me anything about the car that might help me find that kind of car?"

"No!" was all that she could answer. Harry realized that Marge, in the short period he'd questioned her, had given him nearly as much information about the case as he'd collected on his own through evidence and lab reports. With each piece of the puzzle being fit into the picture, however few the pieces might be, the picture was beginning to enlarge. "Marge, you said a moment ago you didn't own a gun like that. What kind of gun did you see?"

"A pistol!" She said quickly.

Harry sat quietly looking over his notes as the two women spoke softly to each other. Several moments passed, then Harry spoke up. "Is there anything you can think of to add to what you've told me?" Marge sat quietly thinking, and as her head began to shake from side to side, Harry felt that what he had was all he'd get. "Well, ladies," Harry concluded in his usual demeanor, "thank you for everything. I'll see to it you're released immediately."

Pat and Marge reached for each other to embrace while Harry, preparing to leave, was organizing his notes. Suddenly, without warning, Marge began to speak. "Harry, there was something about that car."

His eyes became wide, and sparkled in the glare of the overhead light.

"That car made a clacking noise when it pulled away." The wonderment on Harry's face seemed bewildering to both women.

"What do you mean...a clacking sound?"

"Clacking...clacking. Clackity-clack, clackity-clack. It made that sound." With that said, Marge turned and began gathering her things to leave.

## CHAPTER 13

$I$RENE'S HOME WAS BUILT ON THE TOP of a gradually slopping knoll. Its manicured lawns surrounded many keenly placed flower beds, displaying a multitude of color. The smooth black-top drive allowed a visitor to traverse in a semi-circle over the entire front half of the property. The house, with its gray cedar shingles so characteristic of the homes in the coastal area, was partially concealed by an assortment of large weeping willows on its west side, and several towering blue spruce on its southeastern side. The grounds exemplified the very meaning of solitude.

During the short drive over the grounds, Harry seemed calmed by the colorful kaleidoscope, and he welcomed the silence that seemed to emanate from the grounds themselves. As his vehicle entered the final gradual turn, he saw Irene almost fully reclined on a wood-framed deck chair, partially shaded beneath the matching lawn umbrella. Harry frowned slightly, surprised that despite the nearness at which he'd driven his vehicle to where Irene was seated, she made no outward sign that she noticed. He stepped from the vehicle, but did not slam the door.

"Ms. Young," he called out softly at a distance of several feet, but again there was no response. As he approached and faced her, the sun glared from her very dark sun glasses, revealing slightly the outline of her closed eyes. On the wooden arm of the chair sat a half-finished drink and he wondered from the color if it was alcohol. He took a half-step forward, and as he reached out to nudge her arm, the open, empty pill bottle became visible under the chair.

In a very loud voice, Harry began calling her name. "Irene, Irene!" and shaking her as if he would dislocate her shoulder, yet there were no visible signs of life. He took her wrist quickly, and felt a pulse so slight that to an untrained hand it would be imperceptible. He placed her hand down gently across her lap, running quickly to his car and the radio. He called the dispatcher and requested an ambulance, giving directions to the residence. Upon completing his call, he raced to the trunk of his car, pulled out a blanket, and returned to Irene in an attempt to comfort her as best he could until the EMTs arrived.

He stood over her in near disbelief, rubbing her arms in an attempt to revive her circulation. Her breathing was shallow, but she was still breathing, and she continued to maintain a pulse; therefore, he thought, he would not need to administer CPR. "Thank Christ for that," he said softly. In the distance, he now heard the low wail of an approaching siren. For Irene's sake, he hoped everything would go well, but he could not shake a strong feeling of apprehension about the developments surrounding this case. "What the hell is going on here?" he said at just above a whisper. "This woman tried to kill herself."

## CHAPTER 14

HARRY STOOD SILENTLY, watching the red strobe lights from the ambulance as it wound its way over the curved driveway. "Where the hell is all this going to end?" he said to himself. He laughed slightly. "Oh, Christ, my mother told me it was only the crazies and the rich who talked to themselves, and I know I'm not rich." He watched the EMTs work on Irene then lift her into the back of the ambulance. He returned to his car after the ambulance had disappeared, and called dispatch. "It's Harry Circus here. I'm in Berryville at Irene Young's house. I need to get through to Sgt. Barnes. I'll wait here." No more than two minutes passed before Sgt. Barnes' voice rasped through the speaker.

"Harry, having a busy week, are we?"

"You could say that."

"What have you got?"

"I've got a bunch of pills and booze swallowed here. I need to check around, see what I can find."

"It's a little late," responded Barnes, "but I think I can get in touch with the judge and have a search warrant over to you in about an hour."

With warrant in hand, Harry entered the home through a side door located at the end of a hedged walkway. He found himself standing in what appeared to have originally been the mud room, instantly stirring memories of a similar room in his grandmother's home where the jackets and hats of winter hung on hooks above the wearer's slightly wet boots, leaving all soiled outerwear far from the cleanliness of the rest of the home. It was a room that collected the aromas from the kitchen, entrancing anyone entering from the outdoors.

Harry glanced quickly over the contents of the room, and noticed that everything had its place. He found the kitchen, dining room, living room, and study to be impeccably clean and in order. He climbed the stairs to the second landing, glancing quickly through the opened doors at the finery displayed in the well-furnished guest rooms. Upon reaching the largest of the upstairs rooms, Harry knew he'd found Irene's.

This large bedroom, surprisingly enough, appeared to be from another world. The entire room was in total disarray. Clothing was thrown everywhere. Wrinkled clothing was stacked on chairs, dressers, even on the floor in one of the corners. Skirts and dresses that had been worn were left where they fell after being removed. A large mirrored bureau, the top cluttered with jewelry and perfume bottles, was positioned so that anyone lying in the bed had a complete and unobstructed reflection.

"Um," Harry moaned, as his head began to swivel in a kind of naughty approval. He walked slowly through the room, scanning the tops of tables and chairs, hoping something would become visible that could somehow shed light, if only a flicker, on this baffling investigation. Nothing, however, could have prepared him for what he found in the large walk-in closet at the far end of the room. Before him, grinning from ear to ear with an erection the size of Hancock Point was a full-length, life-sized nude photograph of Lester Sawyer tacked to the wall. Harry stood dumbfounded, noting a wild, lascivious look in Lester's eyes that he'd never seen and then suddenly noticed an envelope pinned to the area of the photo directly over Lester's left hand, as if he were holding it. Harry stepped slowly toward the photo, taking the envelope between the thumb and forefinger of his left hand and gently removing the pin with the thumb and forefinger of his right. "Now," Harry murmured, "I've seen everything."

Eyes still focused on the photo, Harry walked slowly backward away from the photo, then turned toward a small corner desk and chair. He sat heavily in the chair, looking back at the photo. He wasn't concerned with the nudity; his dismay was the subject of the nudity. This was a long-time friend of strong community character, and the photo uncovered the dark side of a man who'd led a double life. Memories from the years he'd known Lester flashed through his mind, followed by unwanted images of Irene and the Lester in the photo on the bed in front of the mirror. "And you think you know someone." Harry spoke the words softly as his eyes turned downward to the envelope he held in his hand. It was not sealed; the flap was merely tucked in. He paused after pulling the flap, wishing it was someone else who'd found all this, and with dread he removed the contents of the envelope and began reading.

*"What the hell does it matter? Without Lester, I have no life. I don't care who knows now. Tell everyone we're going to be together again. Not even Betty can stop us now. She never wanted him until she found out about me, then she wanted him back. Go to hell, bitch!"* Harry was stunned at how blunt and callously the note was written. It was void of any feeling or sorrow for what she was about to do to herself. Of the entire note, six words seemed magnified

in his consciousness, leaving him feeling empty to the pit of his stomach. Were these merely the words of a despondent mind? Or was this conjecture on his part about the feelings of a woman's scorn? He needed time to think. Things were happening too fast now. *"Get away for a while,"* he thought to himself. Looking around the room, he saw the telephone on a bedside table. Going directly to it, he dialed his number. He stood quietly as the calling tone chimed in his ear. "Hello, Circus residence."

"Annie."

"Hi, where are you?" she asked with a tone of concern.

"I'm at Irene Young's, and was wondering if I might pick you up." Annie knew from the tone of his voice that something was wrong.

"Harry, what's happening?"

Harry interrupted. "Can I pick you up?"

"No problem, I'll be watching for you."

"Fine, I'll explain everything then. Love you."

"Love you too." She replied.

Harry placed the note into the envelope, then walked to the closet containing the photo. Without looking in, he closed the door.

—

Harry drove his usual foot-to-the-floor speed after leaving Irene's driveway. He had one thing in mind…picking Annie up, taking a short ride to unwind and make plans for what was left of the weekend, and to rest and sort things out. It was a short drive to his home. Annie was outside waiting as he turned into the driveway. She greeted him with a kiss while the vehicle remained idling in park. They sat quietly looking into each other's eyes.

Annie could feel his frustration. She smiled gently, and said,

"Are you going to be all right?"

Harry ignored the question and said, "We need to get away for a while. I need some time to think. I thought we might head out to camp for the rest of the weekend."

Annie smiled. "That sounds great to me." Harry placed the gearshift into reverse and backed out of the drive. As the vehicle entered the roadway, it was as if a switch turned on, and Harry began unloading every ounce of frustration that had built up within him since the discovery of Lester's body. It was now that he told her of Irene Young's attempt on her life. Annie, looking directly at her husband and listening carefully, remained very still. Harry continued driving and talking with no apparent direction planned. After some thirty-odd minutes of driving, he seemed to be regaining a normal frame of attitude. Annie was now able to get in a comment or two that seemed to be registering. He suddenly looked at her and said, "Christ, have I been rattling on or what?"

"No problem, Harry," she replied. "If you can't rattle on with me, who can you rattle on with?" They looked at each other and smiled. Harry turned north on a road that would take them back to Berryville.

## CHAPTER 15

THE DARK-HAIRED JUDGE SAT SOLEMNLY reading over the documents before him. Seated below and to the judge's right, breathing and exhaling deeply to the point of being annoying, was Davis Norton. In the area reserved for court officers and police, the rigid forms in uniform sat, awaiting the announcement of the cases that had brought them here. A court-appointed lawyer directly at Davis's side occasionally spoke in whispers to his client. In high-pitched tones, Davis would respond, "Yeah, yeah, yeah," or "No, no, no."

The judge, visibly disturbed, looked up several times, yet said nothing. Harry Circus, still passive after a wonderful weekend with Annie, seemed oblivious to what was taking place around him. The judge cleared his throat, then ordered the clerk to read the docket. As he did, the judge focused a cold stare directly toward Davis, and in response, Davis focused his stare at the judge.

The judge asked Davis and his attorney to stand before the court, then the charges being leveled against him were read, and he was asked how he would plead. As his attorney began speaking, he was abruptly interrupted by a belligerent and almost out-of-control Davis. "I'm fuckin' guilty as a big-ass crow peckin' corn, and all you goddamned fools know it."

The lawyer motioned for him to remain calm, but Davis rambled on. "Don't think I'm gonna sit here listening to a line of shit from a young punk lawyer. I cut that prick up and I'd do it again!"

"Come to order!" The judge hollered. "Keep that man quiet. Mr. Norton, if I need to have you removed from this court, I'll do it, but I will make a decision in regard to you today."

Davis continued his barrage of profanity in the judge's direction, and was finally removed, kicking and swearing at the Court Officers who'd cuffed him and dragged him from the courtroom.

With the courtroom finally settled, the judge ordered it cleared of anyone having nothing to do with the case. A lengthy discussion ensued between the District Attorney and the court-appointed lawyer to consider all of the charges against Davis in relation to his present state of mind. Finally, the judge ordered him remanded to the state mental health facility at Bangor for psychiatric evaluation.

—

Outside, the court building was buzzing with TV reporters—crews stretching cables in every direction, positioning themselves in order to be first as the D.A. or any police that might have anything to do with the case exited with a rundown on the proceedings. Over the weekend, rumors had spread about Irene Young's suicide attempt—which had left her in a coma—and reporters wondered if she might somehow fit in with this murder investigation. The public had questions, and now it wanted answers. Until this point, the authorities had maintained a no-leak investigation. For that, the D.A. and the State Police had much to be thankful for, but a statement was in order, and well overdue.

Harry had been smart enough to leave by the building's back door, and when the D.A. stepped out of the front door, his befuddled expression reflected his annoyance at standing alone before the media reporters and their cameras. "Shit," he said softly so his words wouldn't carry to the ears of the waiting crowd. Displaying his best political pearly whites, he advanced, ready to field questions from an eager press.

Wanda Lane from Channel 2 News was first. "Is it true, sir, that two people have been arrested in connection with the Lester Sawyer murder investigation, and is it true that one has been arraigned here today?" The D.A. cleared his throat.

"First, a local by the name of Davis Norton has been remanded to BMHI for psychiatric evaluation." Wanda interrupted him.

"Is he your prime suspect as murderer?"

"Uh, no, actually. Mr. Norton has confessed to the desecration of the body as it was found on the blueberry barrens, but vehemently denies having had anything to do with the actual murder. Now, in response to your second question, there was a second person detained, but that person has been released." Thinking to himself that this would be the perfect opportunity to make a move toward his waiting car, he was stopped cold once again by Wanda.

"Well, excuse me sir, but is the state satisfied with Mr. Norton's confession?"

"Uh, probably to this point of the investigation; however, lab tests on some particulars taken from Mr. Norton's home are incomplete. Therefore, I cannot comment further where it involves Mr. Norton."

From the rear of the crowd, another question came. "Was the

other person being held male or female?"

"No comment," replied the D.A. as he began clearing a path to his car. Anticipating his departure, the questions came in a barrage, but he merely held a hand up to each one and replied, "No comment." The reporters followed, bringing him to a near-run. He reached for the door, pulled it open, and jumped in. The questions were still being shouted in his direction as the car pulled away.

—

In a darkened room at Eastern Maine Medical Center where Irene had been transferred because of the seriousness of her condition, Harry Circus stood, erect and silent, watching the faint movement of the blanket that covered her while she breathed, lying motionless in a coma. After a few moments, a young nurse entered. She seemed startled at first, but upon recognizing the trooper, she smiled and approached slowly.

"I didn't realize she had a visitor."

"Yes," replied Harry. "I'm sorry...I forgot to check in at the desk. I've had a lot on my mind lately."

"Oh, no problem, I'm sure," the nurse said. "But unfortunately I don't think she'll be much company. Her condition hasn't changed since she arrived." Harry sighed, but said nothing.

Harry and the young nurse conversed for several minutes, as she was pleasant and a good conversationalist. Finally, Harry looked at his watch and realized the distance he must cover before his day would end—peacefully, he hoped. He jotted several telephone numbers on a piece of paper, asking the nurse if it were possible to leave the telephone numbers where he could be reached day or night in the event there were any changes in Irene Young's condition. The nurse took the piece of paper with the numbers and placed it on Irene's chart at the foot of her bed.

Harry thanked her, leaving quickly.

He sat in the hospital parking lot for several minutes looking over his notes of the day and the past week, realizing that at this point he was no closer to solving the case than he had been a week ago. His only real lead was a car that went clackity-clack. He shifted the car into drive, and eased his way through the parking lot, merging with the flow of traffic in the street. He headed east for a long-awaited visit with Betty Sawyer.

—

Harry pulled his vehicle into Betty Sawyer's drive at just a little before 1:00 p.m. He thought back for a moment to the morning he'd brought the bad news to her, and her reaction to it. In a blur, the events of the past week flashed before him, making him uneasy. He looked down, assessing the condition of his uniform after spending the last several hours driving, then got out. He put on his Stetson, straightened his tie, and walked directly to the door. He lifted the hinged brass arm slightly, bringing it down twice solidly.

Stepping back, he focused on the odd shape of the knocker. It was molded to form a closed fist and forearm hinged where an elbow should be. The knuckles pounded squarely on what appeared to be a protruding, very pronounced cleft chin. Harry, considering the type of man he thought Lester actually was after finding the blown-up photo in Irene's closet, was not surprised in the least with the configuration. What did set him back, however, was until now he'd never noticed the knocker before. Harry heard footsteps approaching from inside, and with the clicking of the lock, the door opened. Standing before him, looking like death warmed over, was a bathrobe-clad Betty Sawyer.

"Oh…hi, Harry."

Looking her over from top to bottom, Harry responded softly, "Good afternoon, Betty."

"Please come in, Harry, just don't look at the house. It's a frightful mess."

Harry looked around and responded in an undertone, "That's an understatement."

"What?" Betty asked.

"I said, I understand."

"Please, won't you sit down, Harry?" And, immediately upon Betty saying the words, they both looked around, finding absolutely nowhere to sit. The entire room was in total disarray. There were half-eaten sandwiches on the coffee table and armrests of chairs, and empty beer cans strewn everywhere, which shed some light on Betty's present condition.

"Betty, what in hell is going on here? This isn't like you."

Betty said absolutely nothing. She merely stood looking at Harry with a lopsided grin, then she spoke. "Look, Harry, I haven't been through a picnic, you know! I haven't felt like doing anything, so I haven't."

"Well, I can see that." Harry responded.

"Why don't we go into the kitchen, and I'll make some coffee. We can talk there, okay?" They both stepped over the debris and went toward the kitchen, trailed by a TV announcer's voice: "This is an elegant 14-karat-gold Herringbone necklace, and you can get it right now, only from the Home Shopping Network." Both Harry and Betty appeared very uncomfortable as Betty made coffee and the Mr. Coffee gurgled out its finished product.

"How do you like it, Harry?"

"I'll take it like you pour it."

"Ohhh!" responded Betty, rattling on that she could never drink it black and how she needed at least one sugar or one pack of sweetener and a little milk or cream. Harry, looking into his steaming cup after it was filled, said nothing, but couldn't help wonder if the cup was clean. After a few moments and half a cup, the caffeine began to take effect on Harry's empty stomach. He stirred restlessly, taking out his notepad. Considering the condition of both Betty and the house, he knew small talk would do nothing for either of them.

Harry breathed deeply, exhaled, and began questioning. "Would it be a problem for you if we went over the day of the murder?"

"I don't think so, Harry. I can handle it," responded Betty.

"I'd like to start at the very beginning of the day. Can you recall how that day started?"

"Well, Harry, it started as usual, you know, coffee and a little breakfast, nothing different."

"What about phone calls? Did anyone call that morning?"

"Let's see, um, the kid that mows our lawn called to tell us he'd be here late in the afternoon. Lester left for the bank at his usual time. I did a little cleaning up around here," she said, looking around as she spoke, "and otherwise, same old, same old." Betty grimaced while glancing again at her surroundings.

"It would be safe to assume, then, that Lester worked all day?"

"Yes, we met here, oh, let me think," she said as she tugged lightly on the lace collar of her robe. "Yes, it was around three-thirty when Lester arrived and I gave him the surprise news." She looked down to the floor, then back up to meet Harry's stare.

"What surprise news?" Harry asked.

"Yes…I was supposed to be out of town for the weekend, at a charity dinner in Portland, you know. Well, anyway, our plans got messed up, and I thought I'd ask Lester to the VFW dance Friday night."

"Was he surprised?" Harry asked.

"Oh my, yes, we danced all evening." Then reaching into her bathrobe sleeve, she pulled out a handkerchief and began sobbing.

"Oh my goodness, I can't believe he's gone." Harry sat silently, wondering how he could get himself out of this and not make himself look like a real bastard. Betty continued to whimper, as the note pinned to the photo kept flashing in Harry's mind. He thought to himself, *"Could she have known of the affair all along, or was it merely an assumption on Irene's part?"*

"I'm sorry, Betty," was all he could think of to say. He wished Annie were here again.

Within a few moments, Betty had composed herself and told Harry, "I'm all right, if you want to continue."

He cleared his throat. "Did anything unusual happen at the dance, Betty?"

"Well, we did see that awful Davis Norton come in totally drunk, fighting with young William Bradley." Harry's mind brought him back to the questioning of Davis when he had told Harry how he and Irene would have been married if it hadn't been for that little bastard Lester.

"Harry, you seem to be a million miles away. Is everything all right with you?"

Harry laughed slightly, saying "Yes, everything is all right with me. I've got a lot on my mind."

"Well, you should, my word," and with that said, Betty went off on a little talking jig that covered the need to take more vitamins for stress and drink more water, and while her lips moved, Harry never heard a word. His mind wasn't a million miles away; it was in Irene Young's walk-in closet where there was a large blow-up photo, a suicide note, and six little words, *"Until she found out about me."* Harry stared at Betty as she talked, nodding his head occasionally as if listening, "So you see, Harry, the body and mind act in conjunction with the proper intake of what they need."

Harry coughed. "Oh, right, right," thinking to himself, *"This has to be the most simple, happy person in the world, or else the woman has a facade that won't quit."* "Sorry, Betty, but can we get back to that Friday night and the dance?"

"Yes, please do!"

"So, after the ruckus, what did you both do?"

"Like I said, we danced all night, and were among the last to leave."

"Did you come right home?"

"Yes, we had a little wine and went to bed shortly afterward."

"Do you remember approximately what time?"

"It was a little past midnight, Harry." Harry looked over the notes he'd jotted down that evening upon receiving Ralph Bailey's phone call from the barrens. Ralph's call had come through at 3:10 a.m. The autopsy and medical examiner's report indicated that Lester had been killed at approximately 2:00 a.m., and the disembowelment occurred shortly afterward.

"Betty, do you remember when I came to tell you about Lester on Saturday morning?"

"Yes, of course I do."

"Do you remember telling me something about the bank alarm? What was that all about?"

"Well, Lester received a call from the sheriff's department about a security alarm at the bank, asking if he could go down and shut it off."

"Do you remember what time that was?"

"No, but it wasn't too long after we'd gone to bed."

"Is that what Lester told you the call was about?" he asked.

"Yes, he told me to go back to sleep, that he'd be right back." The tears flowed once more, and Betty whimpered almost inaudibly, "And I never saw him again after that."

Harry sat quietly thinking. *"The call Lester received was undoubtedly his summons to death. The person who placed that call had to be Lester Sawyer's murderer."* Harry hesitated a moment, waiting for Betty to regain her composure. Clearing his throat, he asked, "Was everything going well between you and Lester?"

"Yes, why do you ask?" From the pit of his soul, a cold hollow feeling began to creep over his entire body, making him wish he were somewhere else.

"I really didn't mean anything by it. Uh, possibly you've heard of Irene Young's attempt on her life this past weekend?"

Betty suddenly became rigid, gazing in Harry's direction, responding in a sing-song tone. "No, I hadn't! What did she do?"

Harry, evading the question, looked at his watch and rose quickly from his seat. "I appreciate everything you've done to help me, but I must return to Machias immediately." They went to the front door through the debris in the living room, and Harry shook his head as he stepped over a half-eaten plate of French fries smothered in ketchup. Betty opened the door, and as she did, it occurred to Harry to ask. "Oh, Betty, how long has that door knocker been there?"

"I just had it put on yesterday. Do you like it?" Harry merely smiled, nodded his head and walked away.

—

At approximately 4:00 p.m., the intensive care unit of Eastern Maine Medical Center housed a flurry of activity. Irene Young had regained consciousness. Her alcohol/barbiturate-induced coma had lasted only a short period, baffling the medical team assigned to her care. For Irene Young, the real battle was about to begin. She had no immediate family, nor had she any close friends. There had been one close friend in her life, Lester Sawyer. On her patient information chart were several telephone numbers, and only one name appeared at the bottom, State Trooper, Harry Circus.

## CHAPTER 16

HARRY'S EYES SCANNED EACH SIDE of the highway as he drove toward Machias. He never realized how many white four-door, mid-sized cars there were before hearing Marge's statement. His bewilderment, however, originated from wondering how many could possibly clack as they were driven. The report handed to him shortly after completing his interrogation of Marge had shed a much needed light on the investigation. From the time of the murder until now, Harry and his surprisingly valuable confidante, Constable Ralph Bailey, had logged many miles in search of evidence. Harry fervently believed the murderer to be a local who was still in the area, since nothing in the investigation indicated Lester's involvement with anyone from away.

He had narrowed down the description from the lab report on the shattered glass to be that of a specific model, Ford Tempo. That particular type of glass was used in a number of model years, making it difficult to pinpoint an exact year. Unfortunately, none of the major auto glass companies in the area had recently replaced a passenger door window from that type of vehicle. And although no new leads had developed where the pistol was involved, at least he knew it was a .30-caliber automatic. Harry had obtained a computer print-out of all the registered .30-caliber automatics in the state, and the numbers were staggering. *"Reducing the list to the local area would be a fine job for Constable Bailey,"* Harry thought as he pulled into headquarters to sign in.

—

At that very moment, in Berryville, Marge sat in the rocking chair by the window, the very chair that Harvey had sat in when it came time to light his pipe. The breeze was light, but the chill in the air evoked a sense of autumn. Since Marge's return home, Pat had seldom lost sight of her close friend and housemate. On occasion, Jimmy would stop by to see that all was well, and with every visit, he found Marge to be in an unusually quiet and almost polite mood. This morning Pat was in charge of breakfast. She knew that what she was about to offer would bring a smile to Marge's face. It was her favorite—fried lobster in butter—and before she could deliver the plate, she noticed that Marge was grinning from ear to ear.

—

Harry found the message waiting for him when he entered headquarters. Irene Young's personal physician thought it safe now for Irene to be questioned by the trooper. After reading the note, Harry expelled an enthusiastic, "Yes." He left immediately for Bangor. His foot was to the floor as usual, passing through mile after mile of uninhabited forest land followed by unattended blueberry fields where scattered blueberry boxes littered the countryside. The drive between Machias and Bangor would normally have taken between an hour and fifty minutes and two hours. Harry made the trip in a mere hour and thirty minutes.

He entered the lobby of the hospital at almost a run, alerting all who were present to his appearance. He nodded quickly to the receptionist, and entered through the already opened door of the waiting elevator. He felt the slight buckling of his knees from the upward movement while his thoughts raced back to when he'd found Irene, then back to the present and a rapidly climbing elevator. A simple chime rang, the door opened and Harry exited quickly.

The dimly lit, quiet hall gave Harry a sense of security, a calming sensation, forcing him to slow his pace because he didn't want to disturb the patients he knew were resting in the rooms on each side of the hall. He continued slowly but steadily to the last door on the right, and his long-awaited visit with Irene Young. As Harry walked silently through the opened door, the unmistakable aroma of fresh flowers filled the air. Irene's eyes were closed, and from her facial expression, she appeared to be resting comfortably. Harry moved quietly across the room to the night stand beside the bed that held the large bouquet. He picked up the card between the stems and leaves of the arrangement. Scanning the names, he realized the flowers were from bank employees. Suddenly he caught Irene's movement through his peripheral vision, immediately turning his head in her direction. They stared at each other in silence for several moments.

Harry was first to speak. "How are you feeling?"

"Fine," she responded. With that out of the way and a few moments of silence, both Harry and Irene began feeling more comfortable, allowing the conversation to begin and continue smoothly. After several carefully posed questions, Harry informed her that he had searched the house with a warrant after finding her in the condition she was in. Irene hung her head for a moment, then spoke openly and at length about her affair with Lester Sawyer. Harry found himself on the receiving end of a load that obviously became a burden for quite some time. Irene became so emotional that her voice rose, bringing a slight redness to her cheeks and a swelling of the jugular in her neck. Each time, Harry raised a hand motioning for her to be still. She would quiet down, then he would ask a question and she began again.

An hour passed, and soon a nurse looked in, her face suggesting concern, but she said nothing and left. Harry looked at his watch, surprised at how rapidly the time had flown by. He was convinced of the relationship by the speed at which Irene spoke. None of it was made up. The conversation was rapidly approaching the day Irene tried to take her own life, the day Harry walked into a world he never knew existed. He was trying to figure out how to approach the subject of the large photo when suddenly, Irene began talking about the photo herself.

"I'm thinking that you may have found your way to my... walk-in closet and...Lester's photo." Harry nodded his head, yet remained quiet. "We decided to take it as a humorous anecdote to a serious situation," she said.

"You must have known you were both playing with fire." Harry said.

"Yeah, we knew, but neither one of us could end it. Damn it, we fell in love."

She spoke of it in a manner that expelled any thought of perversion from Harry's mind.

He allowed her to continue without interruption as she led her story to the final moments when Harry had found her drugged and very near death. As she did, Harry's thoughts returned him to the large walk-in closet, the photo and the envelope pinned to Lester's image. Harry was ushered back to reality by the sound of rapidly approaching footsteps and a nurse who seemed anything but friendly at the sight of Irene consumed by her uncontrollable tears.

—

As Harry was about to leave the hospital parking lot, it occurred to him that double-checking Marge's statement concerning the clacking sound made by the vehicle behind the bank might not be a bad idea. He made a note to call Ralph upon his return home, sending him to Betty's to check Lester's car. The CID had not impounded it, and had allowed it to be towed to Lester's home after a preliminary investigation at the murder site.

## CHAPTER 17

HARRY'S VISION WAS BLURRED by the incessant pounding from a headache that started at the base of his skull and went to the center of his forehead. The dim light from his desk lamp flowed over his notes as his fingers massaged his temples in a feeble attempt at relieving the pain. The house was still, as it generally was at 2:00 a.m. Annie, fast asleep for several hours in their upstairs bedroom, had no way of knowing the frustration that astounded her husband at this very moment. All the time spent, all the information gathered could only point the investigation in one direction, and Harry knew only too well which path it must follow from this point forward. He wanted to be very sure, but down deep he knew. There were only a few key individuals still to be questioned, and in his gut he could feel the slamming of a steel door in the face of a murderer.

Hours later, the early autumn sun rose slowly, giving it the appearance of an angry red planet on the eastern horizon. The droplets that formed on the window from the sun's earliest warmth began dissolving the light coating of frost left from a chilling Maine night. The trooper tried desperately to darken his room, thumping a pillow over his head, but to no avail. He was having another sleepless night. Remaining under the covers became impossible as the aroma of freshly brewed coffee filled the room from a warm kitchen below. Before he reached the coffee pot, his mouth formed a snarl at the sound of the telephone ringing from the sun-filled room at the end of the hall. Annie, who'd been enjoying the natural warmth of the room, picked the receiver up before the finishing of the first chime. It was the D.A., and it wasn't a social call. His voice was brusque. "Is Harry up?" Annie handed the phone to Harry.

"Good morning, trooper. How are things going for you?"

"As well as can be expected, sir."

"Well, I'd like it very much if you could stop by my office today to discuss the Sawyer investigation."

Harry responded quickly. "I sure can. In fact, I was planning on calling you later for the same reason."

"Have you turned something solid, Harry?"

"Let's just say something has turned me." With that said, both men hung up simultaneously. Harry turned, walking toward the kitchen, mumbling softly as he went. "I need coffee."

—

Harry had barely put down his first cup when Constable Bailey's car pulled into the driveway. Annie, who was seated across from her husband, looked up quickly in an attempt to study his facial reaction to the early-morning goings-on, but it was as if Harry hadn't noticed the vehicle. He remained perfectly still, with both hands wrapped around his coffee mug, his stare focused somewhere on the center of the large maple table. Ralph knocked lightly, and was motioned in by Annie, who greeted him with her usual smile and a cordial good morning, handing him an already poured cup of the brew.

"Good morning," chirped the constable, accepting the steaming cup. Getting no response from Harry, he sat quietly in the chair beside the trooper. Several minutes passed; the silence in the room was unnerving. Harry remained quiet throughout his second cup. Annie and the constable made chit-chat out of some tidbits of gossip.

The first word out of Harry's mouth was, "Good morning."

Ralph responded, "Shit, you look like death warmed over."

Harry grimaced, gazing at the constable through the corners of his eyes. "Were you able to get any help with the info we needed on the .30-caliber automatics owned by locals?"

The constable went into detail about the places he'd been and the people he'd talked with, and offered Harry a complete rundown on paper of local residences owning .30-caliber automatics. Harry sat quietly looking over the list of names, as Annie watched her husband at work. She loved watching his intensity when something seized his interest, and hoped she would soon be the focus of his undivided attention.

Several moments passed. Harry looked up, shaking his head. "There's nothing here! I may send you out with a few short questions for these people, for the record, but they won't be able to help."

The constable's eyes were riveted in the trooper's direction, yet he remained quiet. Harry spoke up a bit louder. "What about Lester's car? Did you get over there?"

"Well, Harry, I never got a chance to even get into the garage. Betty told me she sold the car last week—a fella' from Connecticut came up and took it away. She said she let it go for a song and a dance, just wanted to get rid of it."

"Is that what she told you?"

"Damn near word for word." Harry looked inquisitively toward Annie as if searching for a reason, but merely found a similar expression from her, facing him.

—

It was shortly before 10:00 a.m. when Harry arrived at the District Attorney's office. Walking through the large oak door, he felt a coldness in the lack of expressionism in the room's design. The antiquated portraits of former District Attorneys hung on faded yellow, semi-gloss painted walls that were in need of freshening up. The curtains appeared to have been hung by the original D.A., and it was anyone's guess when that might have been. Even the huge desks with ornate carvings were outdated, but they apparently served the purpose.

He thought, *"This is not an office to come to relax in";* however, he shuddered to think how anyone could spend eight hours a day working here.

The receptionist greeted him, motioning for him to proceed in the direction of the D.A.'s private office. As he drew near the partially opened door, the tone at which the D.A. was already speaking gave the trooper the notion to hold back from entering, not knowing if the subject of the clamor was present inside the office. As he neared the inner office, he was motioned to come in by the D.A., who was speaking on the phone. Harry sat in the oak chair opposite the large desk, and the D.A. immediately ended the telephone conversation.

"Harry, glad you could make it so quickly. The press is eating me up on this thing. I'm running out of back doors, if you know what I mean."

Harry, nodding his head in agreement, thought wryly of the

comment, thinking to himself, *"Who the hell's the politician here?"* The conversation continued as the D.A. paced back and forth, finally making his way to the door and closing it. Harry gave him a complete rundown on everything he and Ralph had accumulated as information or evidence, some of which the D.A. had already become familiar with. Eventually, Harry began to offer his own gut feeling about certain incidents and events, which gave him reason to consider questioning several individuals further. The D.A. remained silent throughout Harry's analysis of his findings.

Finally, when it became apparent that Harry was experiencing intense emotions, the D.A. offered his suggestion. "Harry, I want you to go ahead with your investigation; however, let me caution you to proceed very carefully. I don't want the final nail pulled on us."

Harry spent far more time with the D.A. than he'd hoped. The D.A.'s support, however, was crucial in continuing the investigation with as little evidence as was turned to date. As Harry drove toward Berryville, he compiled mental notes as to how he would proceed.

## CHAPTER 18

THE PAVED WALKWAY LEADING TO THE BANK'S ENTRANCE was lined with an assortment of bright, multi-colored annuals that maintained their brilliant color throughout the fall season to the time of a killing frost. Usually such a frost settled upon the area around the end of September. It was now October, and no such frost had hit as of yet, making it a most unusually warm autumn. Harry parked his vehicle at the curb centered on that walkway, making it completely visible to anyone in the bank.

As he entered the bank, he was greeted with simple nodding from the tellers, who were preoccupied with their respective customers. Noticed by the new branch manager, Harry was approached and greeted warmly by the younger woman who'd filled the vacancy made available by the death of Lester Sawyer and she directed him to her desk. She was the manager of the Bangor branch of the same institution. It was a temporary arrangement, until a permanent replacement was found. After a few moments of small talk, Harry explained his reason for stopping at the bank.

"I'd like to apologize for not calling, but I've been rather pressed for time," Harry explained. "Are all of the tellers that worked with Lester and Irene here today?"

"All except one," responded the manager. "Darcy Richards is on a leave of absence for a time. As you may already know, her mother is rather ill, and it's been placing a real burden on Darcy."

"I don't know her all that well," responded Harry.

"I didn't really get to know her either, since she applied for the leave very shortly after my arriving here at the branch."

"If it's at all possible," Harry asked, "I'd like to interview your tellers one at a time. Just routine stuff, I might add. I met with them shortly, following the...." Harry paused, having a difficult time saying the word, "Murder."

"Oh, of course," responded the manager. An uncomfortable silence fell between them as she struggled to find a soft spot in the chair. "I'll clear a place in the employee lounge. Take all the time you need." Harry thanked her and followed her toward the lounge. There were three tellers on duty, and one by one they met with Harry. Each had been questioned earlier, as Harry had indicated. The questions at that time had been generally focused on people and events associated with the branch office.

This time, however, Harry's questions were specific. Who from the bank was aware of the relationship between Lester and Irene? Was there anyone else involved with either Lester or Irene, and were there any confrontations between the two, or with anyone else? As the questioning continued, it became clear that everyone at the branch knew of the affair, and at some point all had taken part in a humorous ridicule of the manner in which both Lester and Irene had conducted themselves at the bank on several occasions.

After completing his interview with two of the tellers, Harry felt this would end as he'd predicted in his mind. There wasn't anything added to what was uncovered previously. He was surprised that the employees had found humor at the unprofessional behavior Lester and Irene had displayed to lower-echelon employees.

The youngest of the three tellers now made her way into the lounge. Her schoolgirl smile and obvious youthful appearance seemed somewhat out of place in this predominantly middle-aged, straight-faced office. She looked rather stunning, Harry thought, as he watched her walking toward him in her long, floral print dress that buttoned up the front. It fit snugly around her slender waist, accentuating her petite breasts. Harry, finding it difficult to stop smiling, greeted the young woman as she sat herself graciously in the chair opposite him. He was entranced by her quiet manner, finding it so much like his own true love, Annie, when she had been nearly the same age.

He cleared his throat and began. "I'd like to ask you a few questions about Lester Sawyer, if you don't mind."

"Not at all," she responded.

"Were you aware of the relationship between Lester Sawyer and Irene Young?"

"Yes, I was."

"Did you know of anyone else involved with either of the two?"

"No, I didn't."

The next question seemed to take even Harry by surprise, as he wasn't sure why he even asked it. "How did it make you feel? I mean, the two of them carrying on that way at the bank here?"

"I thought it was rather sickening, and so did Darcy. We felt so sorry for Mrs. Sawyer. We assumed she knew nothing; at least she never let on when she came into the bank. I think that's why Darcy had offered to help Mrs. Sawyer out after the funeral. You know, run some errands, help to clean the house."

*"Clean the house?"* Harry thought. His-all-too-vivid memory of the condition of Betty's place and the uneaten food in plates left everywhere was rather puzzling to the trooper when held up against this young lady's statement. "Did Darcy tell you this?"

"You mean about helping Mrs. Sawyer and all?" Harry nodded in the affirmative.

"Yes," the young woman responded.

"Have you seen Darcy recently?" Harry asked.

"No, I haven't. We spoke on the phone, let me see, oh, a week ago. She told me she was quite busy with her mother and Mrs. Sawyer."

Harry made a final entry into his notes, thanked the young woman for all of her help, then rose and escorted her to the door. He returned to his chair and began to ponder the notes before him, realizing how little of it made much sense. Momentarily, the branch manager appeared at the door, offering the trooper a steaming cup of coffee. He sat quietly, displaying a peculiar grin, welcoming the opportunity of a needed break.

—

As Harry exited the bank, his vision locked on the constable's car parked directly behind his. Walking to it, he got into the passenger's side. As the door closed behind him, the constable, being his usual jolly-jester self, asked, "Did ya' get it all counted, Chief?"

Harry, straight-faced, breathed deeply, and turning his head slowly toward the constable, responded, "Oh yes, all of it."

Not realizing the seriousness of the trooper's response, Ralph began a hilarious chuckle, which terminated with Harry's sternly asked question, "Did you speak with the people I asked you to?"

Rigid now, the constable responded, "Yes, I did, Harry, and

you were right. They all just seemed rather confused. Some didn't even know Lester outside of what they'd read about him in the papers."

"I thought as much. Ralph, I've got one more stop for you. Get over to Lewbend, talk to Darcy Richards and her mother. This is what I want you to find out."

The trooper explained to Ralph what he needed to know. "I'll be wrapped fairly tight the rest of the day. Check back with me at the house tonight."

"Gotcha," responded the constable. Harry got into his own car, and both vehicles pulled away from the curb simultaneously. There was no doubt in Harry's mind that if something could go wrong, it would. His meeting this morning with the D.A. and their ensuing conversation had given Harry a new feel for the investigation, although many questions remained unanswered. There were several questions running through his mind at the very moment Betty Sawyer's house came into view on the lane in front of him. Harry drove the entire length of the driveway, stopping several feet from the closed, double garage doors.

He remained seated behind the wheel, his stare focusing on the doors themselves. They were made of wood, and designed in a series of square panels recessed in a cross-fitting of frame work, painted white. Suddenly, the trooper realized that the second series of panels from the top, fitted with glass the length of both doors, were now painted over, making it impossible for anyone to see in. He knew the second series was glass because each time he'd stopped here before, he always noticed his reflection was at eye level with that glass. He got out of the car and went to the front door, hesitating as he reached for the queer-looking knocker. He lifted it to its fullest extension and let it drop. It hit solidly, emitting a pronounced metallic rap, then, bouncing once, it rapped slightly again. *"That,"* Harry thought, *"is the biggest, stupidest thing I've ever seen."*

The house was silent within. He turned an ear toward the door, attempting to detect any sound. "I'll be damned if I'm gonna rap that knocker again," he muttered as the distant muffled sound of approaching footsteps became audible. The person approaching, Harry noted, was moving at a brisk pace and heavy-heeled. The latch was released, and the door opened. Standing before Harry was a well-dressed, high-heeled Betty Sawyer.

"Good morning, Harry. What a pleasant surprise."

"Good afternoon!" Harry responded. It was just around noon. Betty opened the door wide and invited the trooper in. As he walked through the doorway, he eyed Betty's attire and wondered whether she was preparing to leave, and asked her as much.

"Why no, I'm not. You know…same old, same old, Harry." Betty began laughing giddily, as if she'd been drinking. Harry's eyes moved slowly from side to side as he saw that the house he'd expected to find in a shambles was as neat as a pin. Everything was in its place. This time, when Betty offered the trooper a chair, it was a welcomed invitation.

After several moments of her hen-like cackling, Harry cleared his throat and politely interrupted. "Betty, if I may? The house looks marvelous again."

"Thank you," she responded.

"I was told you might be getting a little help with it, and I was relieved to hear someone was concerned enough about you to help." Betty made no attempt to respond, displaying an emotionless expression. The conversation proceeded calmly, Harry's keen instinct detecting Betty's apparent discomfort from the very onset of their meeting. He spoke of Davis Norton, leaving out anything that might upset her, yet her only response was that she'd read about it in the *Bangor Daily News*.

"I heard from Ralph Bailey that you sold Lester's car…" As

Harry was about to continue, Betty interrupted coldly.

"What exactly is going on here, Harry? You send that little rent-a-cop out here to see the car. When I tell him it's sold, you come out here and want to talk about it some more. It was my car. If I want to sell it, I can sell it." Harry's cheek muscles quivered at the tone Betty now took.

"I didn't mean for it to be derogatory," replied Harry. Betty's face was expressionless. Her eyeball-to-eyeball stare was unflinching. Harry, who was never intimidated by a stare, returned his own defiant gaze, maintaining his posture until a blinking, shame-faced Betty looked away. Harry paused a moment then spoke again. "Betty, if there's something troubling you I'm a very good listener." Quickly, she responded.

"There's nothing troubling me. I'm simply a little agitated with life in general."

Harry made a suggestion. "I have a very good friend, a counselor..."

"Damn it, Harry! I don't need a counselor. I need to be left alone." Harry's patience thinned. Something was eating at this woman and it was making Harry very uncomfortable. Her agitation was somewhat baffling to the trooper, except for her brief explanation of her desire to be left alone. Harry stood, apologizing with a slight tone of sarcasm for any inconvenience he may have caused, and telling Betty not to get up—that he'd find his way out.

## CHAPTER 19

H ARRY RETURNED HOME at what was normally supper time. Annie was in the habit of preparing the evening meal at the same time each day, regardless of whether Harry called or arrived on time. The past several months however, had found Harry in close proximity to the microwave, re-heating a prepared plate, covered with plastic wrap and refrigerated, awaiting his return in the late evening.

Standing at the door smiling, Annie took much pleasure at seeing her man arrive on time, and the greeting she lavished upon him as he entered seemed to melt them into the very spot. "Are you home to stay?" Annie asked.

"Why? Don't you want me to be?"

"Oh, yes, I do, and if you tell me you are, you better get used to having someone wrapped around you all night long."

"Then—Yes!" Harry said with feeling.

The two held each other and kissed as if they'd never kissed before. Then, they spoke almost non-stop as if they'd been apart for months, like two lovers who'd not laid eyes on one another for quite some time. On several occasions during their conversation, Annie was tempted to reveal her chilled bottle of Chardonnay, but she knew very well that the beverage her husband would desire was coffee. Anything, she thought, as long as she could watch him drink it.

Suddenly, Harry's memory was jogged, and he recalled telling Ralph to check in with him at the house. "Annie." He spoke her name softly. "I...I forgot to tell you something."

With her eyes on her husband, Annie merely tilted her head to one side, expecting the worst. "Ralph will be stopping by, but only for a short time, I promise." Annie smiled as she went to the stove and ladled her husband a bowl of steaming scallop stew. His eyes widened as she placed it before him.

—

The constable arrived well after their meal was finished and they'd retired to the comfort of their living room. The sofa was positioned so as to give anyone seated on it an unobstructed view of the kitchen entrance. Harry was motioning for Ralph to enter as the constable looked in through the glass in the upper portion of the door. Harry had purposely neglected to tell Annie of his encounter with Betty Sawyer, but if she chose to stay in the room with him and Ralph, she would find out because it would come up in conversation.

"Howdy, howdy!" was the constable's greeting.

"Howdy, yourself," responded Harry. Annie smiled on her way past Ralph, asking if he'd like a cup of coffee as she walked toward the kitchen.

"No, thanks," he responded, "the stuff's keepin' me up nights."

The two men made small talk over the events taking place on

the television news. Soon, the trooper, assuming his wife would not return, reached for the remote, clicking the TV off. Harry began by speaking of the manner in which he'd been treated at Betty's. He relayed how quickly her mood had changed from giddy and chattering to defensive and nasty. "Something is eating away at her, and I'd really like to know what," he said.

"Well," Ralph added, "when I stopped there the other day for you, she damn near bit my ear off."

Harry nodded, his face showing curiosity and concern. "I'm probably going to head back over there in a day or two; she may just need a little support." Suddenly, he looked toward Ralph. "What did you find out over in Lewbend?"

The constable relayed the conversation between Adelia Richards and himself, indicating that the woman was semi-bed-ridden and nearly unable to care for her own needs. As the constable continued, several comments he made seemed to captivate the trooper's interest, causing his eyebrows to rise. Ralph continued speaking as Harry's mind half-allowed him to comprehend what was being said, while the other half wove pieces of his earlier conversations at the bank and his short, but intense visit with Betty several hours ago into the mix. Harry refocused himself on what was being said, and shortly the constable offered a tidbit that forced the trooper's eyes wide in apparent surprise. "Her brother-in-law from Connecticut is the guy that bought Lester's car."

—

The next morning, Harry felt rested from his evening alone with Annie. His conversation with Betty and his thoughts about her present state of mind kept up a constant replay in his head. He felt something was eating away at her, and it made him uneasy.

Harry's morning was taken up assisting a young and recently graduated trooper in a domestic violence investigation. With that completed, there was nothing on Harry's schedule for the entire afternoon, making the time prime, he thought, for an extended visit with Betty Sawyer. He needed to know what was making her tick. She was not, in any way, the person he'd once known, nor was her attitude one of a grieving widow.

Harry drove in the direction of the lane on which Betty lived, following the route that wound its way along the river, giving him the opportunity to collect his thoughts. As his vehicle entered a straight stretch of road, giving the trooper a full view of the river, it also provided for him a complete view of the road ahead. Harry saw the pickup ahead of him, and immediately recognized it as belonging to Lennie. Harry had not seen him since the morning he'd discovered Lester's body on the barrens. Several times since the investigation began, he'd wanted to speak with Lennie, but never had the opportunity.

As the distance between the two vehicles closed rapidly, Harry noticed the vehicle operating somewhat erratically. "Shit!" Harry said. "If that old fart is drunk, I'm running him in." The pickup continued another quarter of a mile before Lennie, realizing the flashing blue lights were for him, immediately pulled the truck over onto the shoulder.

Harry walked toward the pickup with a stern face that would have concerned any normal driver who'd been stopped by the trooper. Although when he asked Lennie exactly what he was doing besides driving, Lennie's response was nerve-shattering to the trooper.

"I was just tryin' to see any fish jumpin' in the river theya." Harry inched closer in an attempt to detect any trace of alcohol on Lennie's breath, but found only a foul, unclean odor emitting from the cab, while Lennie grinned from ear to ear.

*"Christ, this guy hasn't washed I'll bet since his mother broke water,"* Harry thought, then stepped back slightly, and for the record asked, "Have you been drinking, Lennie?"

"Not yet," Lennie replied, "but I probably will a little later. Care to join me?"

"No, thanks," responded Harry, "but I would like to talk with you a few minutes, if you don't mind."

"I don't mind," answered Lennie. "I've got all day. Shoot away, Harry." Had it not been for the manner in which Lennie was driving, the trooper would never have stopped him, and the conversation taking place at this very moment, or the information the trooper was about to receive, might never have been brought to light. At some point during their talk, Lennie got out of the cab. Harry returned to his vehicle to turn the blue strobes off, and eventually, both men were leaning against the pickup engrossed in conversation.

To Harry's surprise, the older gentleman was a wealth of information, offering tidbits of this and that covering a wide variety of subjects. He knew of the early involvement between Irene Young and Davis Norton, and how resentful Davis had become toward Lester when he began his affair with Irene, causing the break-up with Davis, the threats Davis had made toward both of them, and his occasional bouts with the bottle. He did not believe that Davis was capable of outright murder, and he told Harry as much.

As the conversation progressed, both men found themselves speaking of Pat and Marge. Lennie indicated he was friends with both women, and had become concerned for Marge's welfare upon learning that she had seen the murder behind the bank.

*"How quickly news travels through small towns,"* Harry thought. He began quizzing the old man in an attempt to find out what might have transpired in conversation between Marge and

Lennie, and as Lennie expounded, Harry realized there wasn't much he didn't know. Finally, Harry asked, "Did Marge tell you about the vehicle behind the bank she says Lester was in when he was shot?"

Lennie responded simply, "No!"

"Well," Harry continued, "we've had a real tough time with it. We still haven't been able to find such a car in the area. We believe it's a late-model Ford Tempo, four-door, white, and there are quite a few around, if you know what I mean." The old man simply nodded. "There was only one thing that may have set this car apart from most. Marge said it clacked as it drove away." Harry coughed a kind of laugh, indicating his frustration.

"Clackity, clack?" responded the old man.

"What did you say?" Harry asked. His facial expression revealed his total interest.

"Clackity, clack! Clackity, clack! I know who owns that car!" Harry's eyes were bulging.

## CHAPTER 20

WITH THE STAGGERING INFORMATION given to him by Lennie—a most unsuspecting informant—Harry felt the breath of new life surging into the investigation. It wasn't as if he were surprised at finding out who might own the white Tempo with the clackity-clack sound. After being a trooper as long as Harry had been, there wasn't much that surprised him anymore. But he was stunned that it had taken this long to uncover it. The words of the D.A. echoed vividly in his mind: *"Proceed very carefully. I don't want the final nail pulled on us."* Proceed carefully was an understatement as far as Harry was concerned. He was filled with vigor; a new excitement pumped through his bloodstream. From the depths of his soul, Harry felt the pounding of that final nail. He notified the Criminal Investigation Division in Augusta that they might follow up on the information on the vehicle and its owner, leaving Harry free to pursue the tiny piece of puzzle he'd been given from one of the bank tellers during his interview.

Harry rehashed almost every question he'd asked Betty

throughout the entire investigation. He remembered thinking to himself that this woman was either the most simple he'd ever met, or else she was a consummate actress. He now believed the latter to be the case. There was no doubt she had damned well known of the affair, and that little note pinned to the photo in Irene's closet was the best indication that she did. The gloves were coming off.

Several times during the investigation, Harry had held fast to the belief that somehow Davis or Marge would slip up, allowing the trooper to prove beyond a shadow of a doubt that one or the other was capable of committing such a hideous crime, knowing very well the volatility of their personalities. Now however, Harry knew. He would proceed carefully, and when he pounded that final spike, nothing and no one would pull it out. Harry immediately got in touch with the D.A. to pass on the new information.

—

Harry pulled into Betty's driveway shortly after noon. The sun was peeking sporadically through large, puffy white clouds blown rapidly eastward by the prevailing winds. The vehicle came to a sudden stop in the center of the drive, blocking the way for anyone that might have intended to enter or leave. Harry exited his car quickly, going directly to the door. He snickered a bit at the knocker, rapping solidly on the door with his knuckles. After pausing for several moments, he rapped again. He stepped back several feet, looking toward the upstairs windows.

After several minutes, it became apparent that no one was in the house. He walked toward the garage doors at the end of the narrow walkway. He made a feeble attempt at gazing through the painted glass. As he was about to leave, the sound of movement from behind the building sparked his interest. Thinking it might be Betty, he continued walking around the building.

Since he'd never been behind the home, Harry was pleasantly surprised at how well cared for the property was. The lawn was well-trimmed, sloping gradually from the building to a small winding brook meandering its way through a cleanly thinned stand of evergreens and white birch, creating a type of fairytale solitude. As he came around the side of the garage, finding no one, he noticed for the first time a rear entrance. He scanned the entire area slowly as he walked, gazing upward occasionally at the building, then back toward the ground.

As he approached what appeared to be a garage door, he saw that the design of this door was identical to the doors out front, and its glass was also painted over. He walked past the garage toward the rear entrance to the house, again rapping solidly with his knuckles on the wooden door. After several moments and no response, Harry retraced his steps through the yard, somewhat disappointed at having to postpone his meeting with Betty. Years of police work had instilled a deep-rooted sense of perseverance in the trooper. Biding one's time was the name of the game.

Suddenly, as he approached the garage door, the sun broke through the clouds, illuminating the entire yard. A reflection at the base of the garage door caught his attention, and he walked directly to it. Harry crouched down and began fingering through the grass, accumulating a small pile of glass. Several feet to his right, he noticed another small area sparsely covered with broken glass. After combining both small piles, he realized how similar these glass particles were to the samples taken from behind the bank and previously sent to the crime lab. He collected every particle of broken glass that he could find, and placed them into his handkerchief. Folding it carefully, he placed it in his shirt pocket. Harry thought, *"This may be just a coincidence, but the lab can decide."*

He walked quickly around to the front, scanning the entire area and seeing nothing and no one, then he entered his vehicle and left.

Harry decided, before his vehicle ever left the lane, that it was early enough for a quick trip to Augusta to hand-deliver the glass fragments to the crime lab himself. Annie's face suddenly appeared in his mind's eye, and he turned the car in the direction for home. This was going to be an official trip, but he was sure that Annie would enjoy the time away, even for a few short hours. He desperately needed her company—needed someone to talk with, someone who'd listen and absorb what he was trying to convey. Although his desire to solve the case was absolute, he could not shake off his feeling of dismay at the possibility of Betty's involvement in all of this.

—

Annie and Harry arrived home that evening shortly after 8:00 p.m. Harry had concluded his business at the crime lab after being told he would have a determination on the glass samples in the morning. They took the coastal route home from Augusta, stopping at Moody's Diner in Waldoboro for the evening's special, turkey dinner with all of the trimmings. The diner brought back many memories for Harry. Both he and Annie were originally from Wiscasset, and they had enjoyed many an evening meal here as Harry was passing through on his way, or returning from his visits with Annie. When he'd been assigned Down East after graduation from the Criminal Justice Academy as a young trooper, they had hastened their wedding plans.

They enjoyed their meal together, and the leisurely drive back to Berryville. Immediately upon entering their home, Harry went directly to the phone, dialing Betty's number. He stood rigidly as the call clicked its way through the exchange. It rang, then rang again, and continued ringing without an answer.

Harry's mind began to work overtime. He hung the receiver

up. His mind raced, going in several directions all at once. "Relax!" he told himself softly so as not to concern Annie, who was visibly happy and relaxed after their day together. He made one final call to Ralph, telling him of his plan, and outlining what he wanted him to do in the morning.

After he'd hung up, he turned to Annie, who looked up at the sound of Harry's approach. They looked deep into one another's eyes, and met in a warm passionate kiss. He felt the warmth of her body. Her breasts pressed firmly against him as he reached for her, running his fingers slowly through the length of her fine hair. His senses filled with the fragrance of her. He breathed deeply as he touched her soft skin, pressing her ever tighter against him. She took his hand and led him to their long-awaited evening.

—

The morning found Harry showered, clean-shaven, dressed, and gulping his second cup of coffee as Annie made her way slowly toward the kitchen.

"Good morning."

"Good morning," she said softly, kissing her husband gently on the forehead.

"Did you sleep well?" he asked.

"Yes, I did." She sat across from him. She extended her hand, and he took it and held it tight.

"This will be over soon," he promised. "Then you and I have to get away for a while."

Annie smiled. "Don't worry, Harry. Everything will work out." His face revealed his true feelings and the effects of the stress the case had placed on him. He stood and walked to the counter where his sidearm and holster lay waiting, and strapped them on. As usual, she shivered inside at the sight of him carrying the gun, and the thought of the danger that followed him every time he went out. She stood as he approached. Neither of them spoke.

They remained unblinking, looking deep into each other's eyes until it was time for him to leave. The big engine roared to a start with the first turn of the key. Harry sat quietly, taking inventory of what information he had, and making mental notes of how he must remain calm during his forthcoming meeting with Betty Sawyer. He knew the lab results of the glass found behind her garage would be crucial as to the direction his questioning would go, but for now, there were a couple of things he would see cleared up. The car rolled slowly forward. Harry caught a slight movement through the corner of one eye. It was Annie waving good-bye. He smiled and returned her wave, then pulled away.

—

The manner in which Harry now drove was a reflection of his determination. His vehicle wound its way over the same route he'd taken when he stopped Lennie and received the information on the Tempo. Suddenly, the vision of Lester Sawyer tied to the wooden rack flashed before his eyes. Then, six words appeared through his subconscious mind as if he were reading them from the windshield of his car, arousing anger within him. *"Until she found out about me."*

As Harry's vehicle entered Betty's long driveway, the new, very large, black Cadillac Deville came into view. It was parked several feet from the closed garage doors. Harry pulled up alongside of it and got out. He walked slowly; eyeing the vehicle, then went to the front entrance of the house. This time, before he could use either the knocker or his knuckles, Betty, who'd noticed his arrival, opened the door and greeted the trooper with less than a "glad-you're-here" attitude. Harry returned the greeting, wide-eyed at her posture as she stood with one arm extended to a middle point on the door, seemingly blocking his way. After an uncomfortable moment, she invited him in. Harry immediately asked about the car, as she directed him to a chair in the living room.

"Yes," responded Betty, "my new Caddy. Do you like it?"

"Very nice!" Harry responded, while displaying his best poker face and thinking to himself; *"Probably paid for with the life insurance money, if and when she gets it."* Rejecting her invitation for coffee, Harry asked politely if she minded him asking a few questions. Betty, seemingly indifferent agreed, and Harry began.

"Betty, how long were you and Lester married?"

"Twenty years," she replied.

"Was it a good relationship?"

"Well, we all have our ups and downs, but yes, it was good."

Harry, detecting slyness in the response, moved quickly to his next question.

"How aware were you of Lester's affair with Irene Young?"

"How dare you accuse my poor husband of such a disgraceful act?"

Harry reminded himself to remain calm, and continued looking straight into her eyes.

"Meaning no disrespect...let me put it this way. If you were not aware of their affair, you were the only one."

Betty's entire physical appearance seemed to swell as if an attack on Harry were imminent, yet she offered no response.

"Well?" Harry asked, his eyebrows rising with the intensity of his stare.

"I don't know what this is all about Harry, but I don't like it very much." Betty was about to continue, but Harry interrupted her.

"Excuse me, Betty, but do you remember the visit I made here when I brought up the subject of Irene's suicide attempt?"

"No...I think so, I don't remember," she said. Harry was searching.

"I found her at her home, very near death. She'd swallowed a bunch of pills and booze. I stayed with her until the ambulance came, then I went through her home in an attempt to find out why this woman would have tried to take her own life, and do you know what I found?"

Not wanting to be crude, Harry reminded himself to not bring up the photo itself. Betty merely shook her head from side to side.

"I found a note written by Irene describing her feelings for Lester, explaining how the affair came about, and including six little words that stuck out from the entire note." Betty's eyes widened in anticipation of what Harry was about to say.

"Until she found out about me," he said.

"What do you think she meant by that, Betty?"

"The woman was obviously deranged," she said simply. "I knew of no affair between my husband and that low-life little tramp!"

At this point in the questioning, a vision again flashed in Harry's mind of the outline of Lester Sawyer's body being wheeled away in a body bag. "Betty, you'd better level with me. I think you damned well knew of the affair, and whatever you're holding back, you'd better spill it now." Betty's gaze was defiant. Neither of them spoke as a sickening stillness came over the entire house. The stillness was finally broken with the recognizable metallic sound of the knocker being hammered on the front door. Both Harry and Betty looked at each other as if searching for a clue as to whom it might be.

Betty excused herself and went to the door, leaving Harry to jot particulars into his notes, but he knew who it was. When she returned, she was accompanied by Constable Ralph Bailey, whose presence was no surprise to Harry. Noticing the large manila envelope the constable carried, the trooper looked at his watch and asked Betty's permission to use the dining room, so that he and Ralph might be alone for a moment.

Several minutes passed. Betty looked up sharply as the two men now re-entered the living room, her hands clenched together. Harry returned to his chair, while the constable remained standing in the archway between the rooms. Harry placed the manila envelope containing the lab results of the glass found behind Betty's on the table in front of him, and handed a search warrant to her which had been issued an hour before.

Suddenly, Betty spoke. "If you don't mind, Harry, I'd like to know what in hell is going on here?" Harry slowly placed his pen on his notepad and neatly aligning the bottom of the pages with the edge of the table.

"Betty, do you own any other vehicles besides the Caddy now?"

Betty seemed taken aback by the question and responded, "No, why do you ask?"

Harry disregarded her question, and moved quickly to another. "Were you out of town yesterday?"

"Ah, yes I was. I went into Bangor to pick up the Caddy."

"The reason I'm asking, Betty, is I stopped by yesterday while you were gone." Betty fidgeted, uncomfortably in her seat opposite him. He continued.

"Strangely enough, the sun illuminated some glass particles in the grass behind your garage. It just so happens they match those taken from your husband's murder scene. By the way…you don't happen to know anyone who owns a mid-size Ford Tempo, do you?"

"That's absurd!" she growled. "You don't know what you're talking about!" Her response appeared to come from out in left field somewhere.

"Don't I?" Harry responded. He stood, turning toward Ralph, handing him the envelope. Harry picked up his notepad and pen, placing them into his shirt pocket. "Betty." Harry's voice now took on a deepness of authority. "I'd like to have a look inside of your garage." Betty seemed frozen to the spot, unable to speak.

Suddenly, Harry's head jerked upward in the direction of the sound of running footsteps from the upstairs portion of the house. Harry pointed to Ralph, ordering him to stay with Betty. He ran through the house following the direction the footsteps had taken, bringing him to the kitchen and the rear door he'd rapped on during his visit yesterday. He figured that the person running upstairs had exited through the back door. Opening the door, he exited into a quiet backyard, and realized the person had exited into the upstairs of the attached garage. He raced around to the front of the house.

He heard the accelerated roar of an engine, and the squealing sound of spinning tires as the garage door exploded in a million splinters of shattered wood and flying glass. Harry's eyes became as round as saucers as he leaped from the path of the rapidly approaching car. He hit the ground rolling, his body smashing against the side of the house. The vehicle was a blur as he struggled to right himself, trying desperately to identify the vehicle. Finally regaining his senses, he saw the vehicle swerve over the grass, digging ruts with its spinning wheels and sending turf high into the air. As it disappeared around the corner of the building, the car emitted a sound that recharged Harry's consciousness: Clackity-clack, clackity-clack.

Harry took off running in an attempt not so much as to follow, but to view the direction the white vehicle took upon entering the lane. It was still unclear to Harry who was driving, but whoever it was seemed to be in total control of the speeding car. As Harry reached his own vehicle, the white Tempo was careening around the final curve at the end of the lane—the same curve Irene Young's car had sped around the night she saw Lester and Betty locked in an embrace the very night Lester was brutally murdered.

Within moments, Harry's more powerful engine pulled his vehicle to within several car lengths of the Tempo. Gripping the wheel firmly with one hand, Harry notified dispatch of his high-speed pursuit, and watched as the speedometer rose above one hundred miles per hour. The chase was leading both cars north on Route 193, the road that led toward old Walter's and the shot-up road signs, away from Berryville and its thickly populated area—for which Harry was most grateful.

Two miles from this very spot however, lay a very treacherous hairpin curve. Harry knew that no vehicle could maneuver through it at these speeds. The insistent pulse of the siren did little to persuade the driver to end the chase, and Harry slowly closed the gap between the two cars. He motioned for the driver to pull over, but to no avail. The miles had closed rapidly.

Harry, realizing what lay ahead, began braking, cutting off the pursuit completely. The driver of the Tempo never slowed, entering the curve at what Harry estimated to be close to ninety. The driver, realizing he or she had reached the point of no return, slammed on the brakes, throwing the vehicle into an uncontrollable skid sideways into the turn. The smoke billowed from the tires dragging across the pavement. The sound of crumpling metal, the explosion of shattering glass, the crack of a splintering utility pole were only a distant "pop" to the trooper's ears, and he arrived just seconds after the crash. He blocked the road at the scene and ran as fast as he could to the aid of the driver.

His shock, however, was overwhelming at the sight of Darcy Richards' body, impaled on the jagged splinters of the utility pole.

—

An hour had passed since the first sound of Harry's voice had been heard through dispatch, informing them of his pursuit and the ensuing high-speed chase. The EMTs had arrived and assumed the gruesome task of removing the lifeless body. The corpse would be transported to Augusta for an autopsy. The demolished remains of the Tempo would also be brought to Augusta and the State Police crime lab, since it was the vehicle described by Marge as the one Lester Sawyer was in when he was murdered. The fact that Darcy had been upstairs at Betty's and her attempt to elude the police, left many suspicions as to Betty's involvement, and Harry wondered exactly how Darcy fit in. He was convinced, however, that Betty Sawyer would be more than ready to discuss all of it with him when he returned.

—

Betty remained seated in the very chair she'd been in when Harry ordered Ralph to stay with her. Both of their eyes locked on Harry as he entered the room, trying to read in his face what had taken place. Harry said nothing. He stood, facing Betty from across the large table. His stare penetrated her very soul, like a bullet from hell. Harry's uniform was filthy, and his shoes were layered in dust, indicating there'd been some sort of confrontation. Betty's gaze, focused on the trooper, was no longer defiant. Her eyes searched anxiously for a facial expression that might suggest empathy for her situation, but saw nothing to indicate such an understanding.

After what seemed an eternity of silence; Harry felt the time was right to begin. "Darcy is dead."

That statement pushed Betty into an uncontrollable hysteria of tears and sobbing. Harry felt something, a sympathy he'd failed to feel for Betty up to this point. Several moments passed. Harry spoke up. "Betty, are you ready to tell me everything now?" She looked toward him, her eyes swollen and red from the tears.

"I don't know where to start?"

"Start at the beginning," Harry said softly, "it's always the best." There was a long moment of silence. Betty appeared to be in some sort of a trance for a moment. Finally, she took a deep breath and spoke.

"Lester and I never really had a good relationship. No matter what I did, it was never enough. It may have been why he felt the need to stray. I could never be the woman he wanted me to be. I did love him at first, or at least I thought it was love. I never knew what love was until I met Darcy."

Harry's eyes squinted as if confused, but he didn't interrupt.

"She'd been hurt far more than I could ever be. For years, I knew Lester had younger women; it was no secret. This is a small town—everyone knew of his goings-on. But he messed up bad—I mean real bad. Darcy saw everything, and she hated him. She taught me how to hate him through her love for me."

Harry was confused and had to interrupt. "Betty, what did you mean when you said he messed up?"

She relayed to the trooper how Lester had raped Darcy's mother more than ten years before, and that Darcy, a mere child concealed in a closet, was a witness, holding the terror of that memory within her all these years.

"Lester never knew, even when he hired her for the bank. It was his affair with Irene that inflamed the hate in Darcy. It was then, when she came to me, that we began to fall in love." Harry slid back on his seat, bringing his posture rigid. For the next several hours, Harry questioned Betty extensively. She held nothing back. She implicated them both in the conspiracy as willing participants in murder.

*EPILOGUE*

———————

SEPTEMBER 11, 1983: The rumors about the Lester Sawyer's murder had stopped long ago, quelled by the passage of time itself. Occasionally it was spoken of at a remote camp on the river, making Lester the butt of a crude jokester. Some however, found it to be less than humorous.

—

Betty Sawyer, convicted of her husband's murder, is serving her twenty-five-years-to-life sentence at the "Max" security facility for women. She never spoke a word throughout the entire trial. Her last words ever were heard by Harry and Ralph when she confessed in her living room, the day her co-conspirator Darcy Richards was killed. Ballistics tests of the weapon found in Darcy's demolished Ford Tempo proved beyond a shadow of a doubt that it was the weapon used to kill Lester Sawyer. The only fingerprints found on the gun were Darcy's.

—

It was completely coincidental how Davis Norton's actions fell into place the night of the murder, taking the heat off the murderers for a time. Davis, eventually diagnosed as a paranoid schizophrenic, has never seen the outside of Bangor Mental Health Institute to this day. His threats toward those he felt were responsible for his fate are a very real part of his everyday life. His voice can be heard echoing those chilling threats through the long empty halls. The lives of everyone involved with this case have changed forever.

Irene Young was never the same. Her endless search for an identity eludes her, and ongoing counseling at times seems fruitless. She retired from the bank. Her gardens provide the constantly sought-after solitude that she needs in order to remain sane.

—

Although Harry dreamed often of escaping from the brutality of his work, he could no more leave the State Police than he could stop fishing and hunting. They were a very crucial part of his life in Washington County, no matter how many times he may have vowed that he would leave, even after Betty Sawyer was incarcerated. In a strange way, he was glad that Marge had not been involved in any way with the murder, but never again would he dismiss the potential of any prospective witness, no matter what their demeanor might be or whatever his first impression of that person was.

—

In some cases, life did not change so drastically. Pat and Marge are as close as ever. Their cabin by the river is unchanged. The long, dusty driveway is still rutted and uneven. The hides of game taken out of season hang neatly behind a false wall in the cool shed, waiting for the price to go up. It never does. They don't need much, as the freezer is always stocked with fresh meat and fish. Jimmy White stops by occasionally. Sadly, nothing ever materialized romantically between him and Pat. However close they became that one time, they eventually understood their true destiny. And the secret that Pat kept, she keeps to this day. Her closeness to Marge, and her need to protect her, was a responsibility that any woman would take for her own sister. Harvey had fathered Pat several years after Marge, but because of Marge's condition, she was sent to live with family who could take care of her. It wasn't until Marge grew up and the family died off that distant relatives sent her back home to Harvey. Pat had grown up with her mother, but Harvey had told her the story, and Pat was sworn to secrecy. Marge's secret would remain with her to the end.

The Wagoneer moved slowly down the gravel road. Evening was settling in; dusk played tricks on untrained eyes. Pat was at the wheel, glancing from side to side. Marge was in the back seat, flipping matches with her forefinger into the ashtray on the door. Her favorite 30/30 Winchester was by her side, a six-pack of Bud at her feet. As the vehicle rumbled onward into the ensuing darkness, the sound of Marge's chant faded into the distance.

"I want to kill something. I want to kill something..."

Keep an eye out for the next installment in the
Harry Circus series,

*Across the Singing Bridge*
by E.D. Ward